"Tell Me The Truth And I Will Love You, Rosalind. I Will Make Such Love To You—"

Her hand flew to her throat. "What?" she whispered.

Najib stroked light fingers down her bare arm. He *was* wounded; she had pierced his heart in the first moment she looked at him, suspicious and mistrustful though her eyes had been.

"You are a woman who enjoys physical pleasure, Rosalind. Do you think a man does not know such a thing?"

She closed her eyes and breathed to silence her noisy heart.

"How my mouth craves to kiss you, Rosalind, my hands burn with wanting to touch you. Do you not feel it? I see it in your eyes. You want my touch. Tell me that it is so. Say it!"

"Najib," she whispered, her body streaming with feeling.

How could such passionate need as Najib felt for her coexist with the deep suspicion that she was a danger—to him, to the family, to the thing that ruled all their lives?

Dear Reader,

Welcome to the world of Silhouette Desire, where you can indulge yourself every month with romances that can only be described as passionate, powerful and provocative!

The ever-fabulous Ann Major offers a *Cowboy Fantasy,* July's MAN OF THE MONTH. Will a fateful reunion between a Texas cowboy and his ex-flame rekindle their fiery passion? In *Cherokee,* Sheri WhiteFeather writes a compelling story about a Native American hero who, while searching for his Cherokee heritage, falls in love with a heroine who has turned away from hers.

The popular miniseries BACHELOR BATTALION by Maureen Child marches on with *His Baby!*—a marine hero returns from an assignment to discover he's a father. The tantalizing Desire miniseries FORTUNES OF TEXAS: THE LOST HEIRS continues with *The Pregnant Heiress* by Eileen Wilks, whose pregnant heroine falls in love with the investigator protecting her from a stalker.

Alexandra Sellers has written an enchanting trilogy, SONS OF THE DESERT: THE SULTANS, launching this month with *The Sultan's Heir.* A prince must watch over the secret child heir to the kingdom along with the child's beautiful mother. And don't miss Bronwyn Jameson's Desire debut—an intriguing tale involving a self-made man who's *In Bed with the Boss's Daughter.*

Treat yourself to all six of these heart-melting tales of Desire—and see inside for details on how to enter our Silhouette Makes You a Star contest.

Enjoy!

Joan Marlow Golan

Joan Marlow Golan
Senior Editor, Silhouette Desire

Please address questions and book requests to:
Silhouette Reader Service
U.S.: 3010 Walden Ave., P.O. Box 1325, Buffalo, NY 14269
Canadian: P.O. Box 609, Fort Erie, Ont. L2A 5X3

The Sultan's Heir

ALEXANDRA SELLERS

Published by Silhouette Books

America's Publisher of Contemporary Romance

for
Jennifer Nauss,
heartbreaker

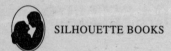 SILHOUETTE BOOKS

ISBN 0-373-76379-4

THE SULTAN'S HEIR

Copyright © 2001 by Alexandra Sellers

Visit Silhouette at www.eHarlequin.com

Printed in U.S.A.

ALEXANDRA SELLERS

is the author of over twenty-five novels and a feline language text published in 1997 and still selling.

Born and raised in Canada, Alexandra first came to London as a drama student. Now she lives near Hampstead Heath with her husband, Nick. They share housekeeping with Monsieur, who jumped through the window one day and announced, as cats do, that he was moving in.

What she would miss most on a desert island is shared laughter.

Readers can write to Alexandra at P.O. Box 9449, London NW3 2WH, England.

SILHOUETTE MAKES YOU A STAR!
Feel like a star with Silhouette.
Look for the exciting details of our new contest inside all of these fabulous Silhouette novels:

Prologue

A heavy, humming silence hung over the ancient brick and modern steel of the bank's safety deposit vault. Three men stood together watching as the manager himself inserted the key that allowed the slender chromium door to open. They exchanged brief glances but no word.

They were young, all around thirty, the manager supposed. There was something about them that he could not place, a sense of themselves, an authority, that was unusual in the young. They reminded him of someone, but he could not say who. Perhaps it was the curiously elusive resemblance they had to one another, some expression in the eyes that made him think their relationship might be one of blood. One had called the dead man, whose safety deposit box he was now opening for them, their cousin.

His fingers hooked into the little handle, and the

bank manager drew out the long, shining drawer. "It has not been touched for five years, of course," he said, feeling somehow that this was his moment. Perhaps it was because they were watching him with such fixed attention.

It was by no means an unusual occurrence in the aftermath of the long and devastating Kaljuk War. Other families had lost track of the safety deposit boxes of their dead loved ones, or had never known of them, until notified by the bank of an arrears on the rental. And sometimes when the bank sent out letters there was no reply at all....

No one answered him, and he slid his left arm under the box as it came free of its sheath. "This way, gentlemen," he said, and turned to lead them out of the vault, leaving a clerk to close and turn the locks of the vault door.

He led them down the narrow passage, on a sudden impulse bypassing the doorways leading to the closets where more ordinary clients of the bank examined their safety deposit boxes, instead going up the staircase to the main floor of the bustling institution.

He headed for a door labelled Meeting Room, and with a nod instructed the young clerk to open it. "You will not be disturbed here," he told them with a certain gravity, leading the way inside.

He placed the box on the polished wood table, then straightened and glanced at the men. Still no one had spoken. Although on the surface the three were completely calm, there was a tension in the air that was of a different order from the usual simple, excited hope that some family treasure would be found to have been saved from the devastation. He wondered what might be in the box.

The bank manager nodded as if to himself. "You will not be disturbed," he said again.

"Thank you," said one of the men, holding the door with polite implacability. Reluctantly, unconsciously wishing to be part of the drama he felt hovering, the bank manager bowed again and left.

Najib al Makhtoum closed the door, shutting him out, then turned to his companions. The three men stood for a moment looking at each other in silence. Strong sunlight slanted through narrow windows high along one wall, casting sharp shadows, and making visible a family resemblance between the three men that was not always so obvious. They all shared some ancestor's broad forehead, strong cheekbones, and full mouth, but each had put his own individual stamp on his genes.

"Well, let's hope this is it," Ashraf said, and as if this were a signal they all three moved to pull out chairs around the table where the box lay, and settled themselves.

A hand reached out and lifted the lid to expose the long, shallow, oblong compartment. There was a collective sigh.

"Empty," said Ashraf. "Well, it was too much to expect that—"

"But he must have—" Haroun began, and broke off as Najib interrupted, "Not empty, Ash."

The other two drew in one simultaneous breath: two envelopes lay flat in the bottom, almost invisible in the sharp shadows.

For a moment they stared in silence.

Najib and Haroun looked from the envelopes to Ashraf, and it was he who reached in at last and reluctantly drew out the two rectangular shapes, one a large brown business envelope, the other a narrow white oblong.

"It's a will," said Ashraf, surprise in his voice. He looked at the brown envelope. "And a letter addressed to Grandfather." He dropped that on the table and turned to the will, starting to unwind the red string that held the flap in place.

"What firm?" asked Najib. "Not old Ibrahim?"

Ashraf turned it over to show the looping logo of a legal firm and shook his head. "Jamal al Wakil," he read, and glanced up. "Ever heard of him?"

The other two shook their heads, and a frown was settling on his brow as Ashraf lifted the flap and drew out the formal legal document. "Why does a man go to a stranger to draw up his will on the eve of war?" he murmured, then bent to run his eyes over the legal phrases.

"Grandfather, his mother..." he murmured, flipping to a new page, and then stopped, his eyes fixed to the page.

"What is it?" demanded the other two simultaneously.

"'To my wi...'" Ashraf read, then looked up to meet the startled eyes of his brother and cousin. "'To my wife.' He was married. He must have—" He broke off and resumed reading as the other two exclaimed in amazement.

"Married! To whom?"

Ashraf read, "'My wife, Rosalind Olivia Lewis.' An Englishwoman. While he was in London. Has to be." His eyes roamed further and he stiffened and raised his gaze over the edge of the paper to fix them with a warning look. "She was pregnant. They thought, a son."

"Allah!" one whispered, for them all. The three men stared at each other. "She would have contacted the family if there was a child," said Haroun weakly. "Especially if it was a boy."

"Maybe not. Do you think he told her the truth before marrying her?"

"Let's hope not."

Ashraf was still reading. He shook his head in contradiction. "He must have told her. Listen. '...and to my son, I leave the al Jawadi Rose.'"

There was another silence as they took it in. "Do you think she's got it?" Haroun whispered. "Could he have been so besotted as to leave it with her?"

"Not so crazy, maybe," Ash pointed out. "Maybe he thought it would be wiser than bringing it back to Parvan on the eve of war."

Najib picked up the other envelope his cousin had drawn from the box. He lifted the flap and drew out the first thing that his fingers found—a small stiff white rectangle. He flipped it over and found himself looking into the softly smiling eyes of a woman.

"It's her," he said.

For an unconscious moment he sat gazing at the girl's face. She was young and very pretty, her face rounded and soft. Looking at the face, he was mostly aware of regret—that five years had passed since the photo had been taken, and that he had not known her like this, with the bloom of sweetness on her soft cheeks...

It was obvious that the man behind the camera had been Jamshid, and that she had loved him. He wondered who she loved now.

"The child will be four years old," Haroun said, voicing the thought all shared. "My God."

"We have to find her. And the boy." Ashraf took a breath. "Before anyone else does. And Haroun's right, he might have left the Rose with her. *Allah,* a son of Kamil and the Rose together—what a prize. Who can we trust with this?"

Najib was still looking down at the photograph on the table, his hand resting on its edge, as though protecting the face from a draft. Abruptly he flattened his hand, drew the little piece of card to the edge of the table, scooped it up, and slipped it into his inner breast pocket.

"I'll take care of it," he said.

One

"Mrs. Bahrami?"

Rosalind stared at the man at her door. It was a long time since anyone had called her by that name. Yet she was sure she had never met him before. He wasn't the kind of man you forgot.

"That is not my name," she said, in level tones. "Why didn't the doorman ring me?"

"Perhaps I mistake," the stranger murmured, with the air of a man who never did. His hair was raven-black above dark eyes and strongly marked eyebrows. Although he wore a tweed jacket and expensive Italian loafers, his foreignness was betrayed by the set of his mouth, the expression around his eyes, the slight accent. "I am looking for Mrs. Rosalind Bahrami."

Rosie's lips tightened. Behind the added years and the different features, there was an unmistakable resemblance. A wave of hostility rose in her, sharpening her senses, so that she picked up the scent of his aftershave. "You—"

"Please," he overrode her urgently, as if sensing that she was about to deny it. "I must find her. Rosalind Lewis married my cousin Jamshid Bahrami some years ago. Are not you this Rosalind Lewis?"

Cousin. Her stomach tightened.

Najib al Makhtoum took in the long, impossibly thick, beige hair, a wave falling over hazel eyes, the slender oval of her face. Soft lips that had once been trusting were set firmly, a slightly ironic tilt at one corner expanding into a challenging half smile now as her eyebrows lifted dismissively. Angry mockery was evident in the curving eyelids too, as she gazed at him. She was not wearing a ring.

"I am," she said flatly, giving no ground. "And it was a long time ago, and as Jamshid's cousin, what do you care?"

He was conscious of irritation. Women did not usually treat him so dismissively.

"I must talk to you. May I come in?"

"Not on your life," she said, with slow, implacable emphasis. "Goodbye."

His hand prevented the door's closing. "You seem to regard your late husband's family..."

"With deep and abiding revulsion," she supplied. "Take your hand away, please."

"Miss Lewis," he said urgently, his accent reminding her with wrenching sharpness of Jamshid. "Please let me speak to you. It is very important."

His eyes were the colour of melted bittersweet chocolate. The full mouth showed signs that the crazily passionate nature was the same, but was tempered with self-control. If Jamshid had lived, probably his mouth would have taken on the same learned discipline by this age, but the memory of the young passionate mouth was all she would ever have.

"What's your name?"

"I am Najib al Makhtoum," he said, with a kind of condescending air, as if he was not used to having to introduce himself.

"And who did you say sent you?"

"I have urgent family business to discuss with you."

"What business?"

"I represent Jamshid's estate. I am one of his executors."

She gazed at him, recognizing a man who would get what he wanted.

"I assure you it is to your advantage," he pressed, frowning as if her reticence made him suspicious.

"Uh-huh." The look she gave him left him in no doubt of what she thought of her chances of hearing something to her advantage from him. "Half an hour," Rosalind capitulated flatly, falling back. She pushed aside a child's bright green wheeled dinosaur with her foot and held the door open.

"Half an hour to the representative of your dead husband's family," he remarked without expression, stepping inside.

"Which is exactly thirty minutes more than they ever gave me."

He took that with a frowning look. "You made an attempt at contact, then?"

She looked at him, not answering. The skin on her back shivered, and she had a sudden understanding of how animals felt when confronting danger. If she were a cat, probably she would look twice her normal size now, her fur standing out in all directions.

But she didn't suppose that that would scare him off. He looked like a man who thrived on challenge.

"Over there," she said, closing the door and lifting a hand to direct him. She watched as he moved ahead of her into the sitting room and towards the sofas at the far end of the long, elegant room. Jamshid had been shorter, a little slimmer. His cousin's frame was powerful, his shoulders broad, strong bones under a firm musculature.

In the bright sitting room Najib glanced around at the resolutely European decor. A beautiful sheaf of white flowers graced the centre of a square black coffee table, with half a dozen little onyx and crystal ornaments. Around it were sofas and chairs, with decorative touches that combined to give the room a soft, expensive sophistication.

Only a couple of pieces gave evidence that she had ever been married to a Parvani—an extremely beautiful silk Bagestani prayer rug in front of a cabinet and an antique miniature of the Parvan royal palace in Shahr-i Bozorg, painted on a narrow strip of ivory in a delicate inlaid frame, hanging on one wall in elegant isolation.

"Sit down, Mr. al Makhtoum," she invited, without pretending to any social warmth. She crossed to a corner of the sofa kitty-corner to the chair she indicated to him. It was only when he set it on the black table that she noticed he was carrying a briefcase.

Rosie was barefoot, wearing soft blue cotton leggings and a long blue shirt. The briefcase suddenly made her feel vulnerable. Unconsciously she drew one bent leg under her, lightly clasped her bare ankle, her gold bracelet watch tumbling down over her wrist, and sat sideways on the sofa, facing him. Her other arm rested on the sofa back and supported her cheek as she gazed at him.

"What can your family possibly want with me after all this time?" Rosalind demanded, curious if not really caring, but a little nervous, too, as he snapped the case open.

"First," Najib al Makhtoum began, "may I confirm a few facts? You are Rosalind Olivia Lewis, and five years ago you married Jamshid Bahrami, a citizen of Parvan who was at that time a postgraduate student at the School of Eastern and Asian Studies here in London?"

"We've been over that," she said. "What else?"

"You subsequently gave birth to his child?"

She went very still, watching him.

"I am sorry to say we learned only recently about your marriage and that you were pregnant when my cousin died," he said helpfully.

"Did you?" Rosalind said, with cool, unconcerned disbelief.

He lifted an eyebrow at her. "Was there any reason, Miss Lewis, why you did not let the family know of the marriage and your pregnancy after Jamshid's death?"

She lowered her head and looked at him under her brows. "I might as easily ask you why Jamshid apparently told no one about me before going off to war," she returned bitterly. "He left here promising to get his grandfather's approval, saying that his family would send for me if war was declared, that I would go to family in the Barakat Emirates and have the baby there…. Well, I guess he never did it. If it wasn't significant to him, why should it have been to me?''

"There is no doubt that he should—"

"In fact, though, as I am sure you know," she went on over him, "I did write a letter to Jamshid's grandfather, shortly after hearing that my husband had been killed.''

She was surprised by the wary look that entered his eyes, but couldn't guess what it meant. "My grandfather died within a year after—" he began, and she interrupted,

"I'm sorry to hear it. I always imagined that one day I would tell him to his face what I thought of him."

"Are you sure my grandfather received this letter?''

She dropped her chin, staring down at the peach-coloured fabric that covered the sofa under her thigh, and felt the old anguish stab her, heart and womb.

"Oh, yes," she said, lifting her head again. "Oh, yes, Mr. al Makhtoum, your grandfather received it, as I think I know. I think you know that he wrote back a charming little note telling me that I was not married to Jamshid, that I was no more than an opportunistic foreign gold digger who could have no way of knowing which of her many lovers was the father of her child, that I should reflect that to receive money for sex would make me a prostitute, and that I would rot for what I was trying to put over on the grieving family of a war hero.

"It was pretty comprehensive," she said, opening her eyes at him. "So what has Jamshid's family now got to add to that?''

Two

It stopped him cold. Najib al Makhtoum looked away, heaved a long, slow breath, shook his head, met her eyes again.

"No," he assured her. His voice was quiet, masking his deep exasperation. Why on earth had the old man—? But it was no use asking that question now. "No, I knew of no such letter. No one did, save my grandfather. Is that indeed what was said to you?"

"Well, it may not be word for word," Rosalind allowed. "You would hardly expect it after five years, though at the time I felt the message had been gouged into me permanently with a dull knife. I suppose Jamshid was lying to me from beginning to end, I suppose to him a Western marriage wasn't worth a thought, but I believed him. I loved him and I believed he loved me and I was pregnant with his child, and to learn so brutally that he hadn't even bothered to mention me to his grandfather was—''

She broke off and told herself to calm down. Railing at Jamshid's cousin would do nothing. And she still didn't know why he was here.

''I am very sorry,'' al Makhtoum murmured at last. ''I apologize on behalf of my grandfather—of all Jamshid's family. The rest of us knew nothing. As I said, we learned of your existence only recently. My grandfather most unfortunately kept your letter secret. It can have been known to none but himself.''

She didn't know whether to believe him, but what did it matter? It only underlined the fact that Jamshid had been faithless.

''Well, now perhaps you understand why I am not interested in anything your family might have to say to me. In fact, I'd rather not have you sitting on my sofa. So—''

He lifted a hand. ''Miss Lewis, I understand your anger. But please let me—''

She shook her head. ''No, you don't understand, because you don't know anything about me or my life, or what effect that letter had. No explanation is necessary, Mr. al Makhtoum. Nothing you could say now would change history. What was it Jamshid used to say? *Makhtoub*. It's written. It's over.''

''It is not over,'' said Najib al Makhtoum softly, but with such complete conviction that Rosalind's heart kicked.

''What do you *want?*'' she demanded.

He coughed. ''As you know, Jamshid died in the early days of the Kaljuk War. We believed that he died intestate, but his will has recently come to light. He left most of his substantial personal property to you and the child.''

Rosalind's mouth opened in silent astonishment. She squeezed her eyes shut, opened them again.

''What?'' she whispered.

''I have a copy of his will, if you would like to read it.''

''Jamshid named me in his *will?''*

''You are the major beneficiary.''

She was swamped by a mixture of feelings she thought might drown her. ''I don't—you—why wasn't I told of this five years ago?''

''We knew nothing of the will until ten days ago.''

''How could you *possibly* not know Jamshid had left a will for five years?''

She sat staring at him, her head forward, her eyes gone dark and fixed on him. He felt the pulse of his masculine ego and was suddenly, powerfully aware of the intensity of her femininity, and understood why Jamshid had married her in spite of everything, even knowing how ferociously their grandfather would object.

''He did not go to the family lawyer, doubtless because he had not yet found a way to tell our grandfather of your marriage,'' Najib al Makhtoum explained. ''He went to a lawyer with no connections to…our family. We have learned that the man was killed and his offices destroyed by a bomb, shortly after Jamshid's own death.''

She had a sudden sharp memory of reading of the bombing raids. How she had wept for the destruction of his country.

She shook her head, fighting back the burning in her eyes.

"Jamshid had put a copy of the will and documents pertaining to your marriage in a safety deposit box we also knew nothing of. The bank sent a routine notice recently when the account that paid for the box went into arrears. Undoubtedly Jamshid had left a key with this same lawyer, expecting the box to be opened immediately in the event of his death."

Rosie pressed her lips together and looked down, her thick beige hair falling forward to provide a partial curtain against his eyes. She sat in silence, absorbing it. A trembling, broken smile pulled at her mouth, and there was no trace now of the bitterness that showed as cynicism. She suddenly looked younger, innocent and trusting. He thought that he was now seeing the girl in the photograph. The girl Jamshid had fallen in love with.

"I see," she whispered again. "That was…" She shook her head, raised her eyes and gazed at the ceiling. Swallowed. "I wish I'd known this five years ago."

"It was not Jamshid's fault that you did not. No one could have foreseen such a tragic coincidence."

Rosalind was shaken to the soul. Five years of her life rewritten in a few minutes. Her eyes burned as the hurt she didn't know she still carried flamed through her. So he had not abandoned her. His love had not been a lie.

Najib cleared his throat. "In the box also was a letter of explanation to my grandfather."

"What did he say?" she asked hoarsely, her gaze on him again.

"I have it here. Would you like to read it?" He reached into his case again, drew out a letter and handed it to her. "I believe you read Parvani? He mentions the fact in the letter."

Her hand shook as she accepted it. The writing swam behind her tears, and Rosalind blinked hard as she read the last words she would ever hear from Jamshid.

"Grandfather, I am ashamed not to have found a way to tell you and the family about my marriage, which took place in England....

"I know that it was your design that I should marry a woman of our own blood, but Rosalind will delight you when you meet her. She is a woman to rise to any demand that fate makes of her, and will be a fine mother to our child, which to my great joy she carries. We think it a son. If it should be God's will that I do not return from this war alive, and that you learn of my marriage through this letter, I trust..."

Tears choked her. She could read no further. Rosalind dropped the letter and buried her face in her hands. "Oh, I wish I had known, I wish I had known!" she cried again. "I thought he betrayed me, I thought..."

She bit her lip and fought for calm.

"He loved me." Her voice cracked. "He did love me."

The stranger with Jamshid's eyes moved and was sitting beside her. "Yes," he murmured comfortingly. "Yes, he must have loved you very much."

"Why didn't he tell his grandfather about me?"

"My grandfather was a man who had suffered great reverses in his life, and for his favourite to have married an Englishwoman was—" He broke off. "For now, comfort yourself with the knowledge that your husband's last thoughts, before going to war, were of you. You and the child.''

His deep, gentle voice tore away the last thread of her control. A cry ripped her throat, and when she felt his arms going around her it seemed natural and right. He was Jamshid's cousin. Rosalind rested her head against the rough tweed of his jacket and wept as the mixture of grief and the deep hurt of betrayal shuddered through her and was at last released.

Najib stroked the long, smooth, honey-brown hair, and thought what a tragedy it was that she had been made to doubt his cousin's love. But there was good reason why Jamshid had not told their grandfather of the marriage....

He remembered the terrible uproar that had ensued when Jamshid came home determined to go to war at the side of Prince Kavian. As one of the prince's Cup Companions, as a man raised all his life in his mother's country, Jamshid had insisted, he must do his duty to that country in its time of need. His grandfather had shouted, had threatened, had told him of his higher duty to his own family, to his father's country and his fate....

The storm of the old man's fury had raged over their heads for weeks, all through the buildup to the first, inevitable Kaljuk invasion, while the urgent diplomatic attempts, one after the other, fell on waste ground. Jamshid had stood resolute through it all, but it had certainly not been the moment to raise the matter of his marriage to an Englishwoman, which his grandfather would have opposed with the utmost bitterness. That might have killed the old man.

So Jamshid, his grandfather's favourite and named heir, had gone off to battle with the old man's curse ringing in his ears, and a few weeks later they had carried his lifeless body back across the threshold, broken, bruised and thin, in early promise of what horrors the war would bring to Parvan. His grandfather had been knocked to his knees by the blow. He never recovered. The change in him had shaken them all. That tower of strength reduced to rubble in an hour.

Rosalind's letter and its revelations must have seemed the final horror to a mind finally driven beyond its limits. Perhaps, in the human way, the old man had turned on her as a way to ward off his own deep guilt. To curse a man going into battle was a terrible thing....

It was a tragedy that he had succumbed to such emotions at such a time. If Rosalind had been taken into the family then, she and Jamshid's child would already be under their protection. But thank God fate had revealed her existence at a time when they could still take steps. Najib thought that it would be his job to protect her now, and his arm tightened around her, making him conscious of the train of his thoughts, so that he deliberately released her.

Rosalind wiped her eyes and cheeks with her fingers, snatched a tissue from the box on the table. She sat up, snuffling, blew her nose, wiped her tears.

"Thanks for the shoulder," she muttered.

"I am sorry to have offered it five years late."

Rosalind shook her head and pulled her still-trembling mouth into a half smile. "Well. What now?"

"I should tell you the contents of his will before anything else, I think."

"All right."

Najib al Makhtoum returned to his own seat, where

he drew the will from his case, flipped over a few pages, and began softly, "Jamshid left you his flat in Paris and another in New York outright. In addition, there is a lifetime interest in the villa in East Barakat to be held by you until your death, in trust for the child. Another property, in trust until the child reaches twenty-one years of age. Certain valuables and some investments intended to provide an income for you." He outlined them briefly, and then said, "The provisions are slightly altered in the case of a daughter, to protect her property on her marriage."

He rested the document on his knees. "Fortunately, none of the real estate or property has been sold in the intervening years. A lump sum payment of the accumulated income is, naturally, due to you immediately."

Rosalind stared at him, her astonishment increasing with every word of this recital. He passed her a list of figures, and she looked at the total he indicated with sheer disbelief.

"Did Jamshid really own all that?"

He looked at her, wondering if her astonishment was genuine. If he really had told her nothing, Jamshid must have been crazy, Najib reflected. But looking at Rosalind, he could see plenty of reason for madness.

"His father died when he was an infant. He came into his personal inheritance at the age of twenty-one. I have taken the liberty of bringing you one of the jewels that forms a part of your inheritance."

He reached into the case, and brought out a small wine-coloured velvet bag. Rosalind watched in silent stupefaction as Najib al Makhtoum expertly pulled open the drawstring and shook out onto his palm a ring. He picked it up between thumb and forefinger, glanced at it, and held it out to her.

It was a diamond as big as all outdoors, in an old-fashioned setting between two pyramided clusters of rubies. It took Rosalind's breath away. It glowed with a rich inner fire, as if it had been worn by a deeply feminine woman and her aura still surrounded it.

"It belonged to our great-grandmother," Najib explained. "She was famed for her beauty, and was a woman of great charm." He looked at Rosalind and thought that he had never met a woman with such feminine impact. Family legend said Mawiyah had been such a woman.

Rosalind stared at the ring. "I don't—are you sure?" she asked stupidly, and, with something like impatience, for she was now a wealthy woman and this ring was no more than a token, he took the ring from her again and picked up her hand.

"Put it on," he said, slipping it onto her ring finger and down over the knuckle, and for a moment reality seemed to flicker, and they realized that it was her left hand. They both blinked and then ignored the fact that unconsciously he had performed the age-old ritual that bound men and women together for life.

They spoke simultaneously, in cool voices. "It's very lovely," Rosalind said, and Najib said, "It's only one of several very fine pieces that are now yours."

She shook her head dumbly. "He never said a word about this. Not a word."

But then, Jamshid had always been reticent about his background. They had dated for months before she even learned that he held the rank of Cup Companion to Prince Kavian.

In ancient times, the cup had meant the winecup.

The companions were the men with whom the Prince caroused and forgot world affairs. But in modern times the position was much more than an honourary one. The Companions now were like a government cabinet.

It was a very prestigious appointment, but Rosalind had somehow not been all that surprised to learn of Jamshid's position. Maybe it was Jamshid's own bearing, or maybe it was that Prince Kavian had always treated his "bodyguards" with the respect of an equal.

Cup Companions to the Crown Prince normally came from the nobility. But Rosalind had certainly assumed, if she thought of it at all, that, like so many other Parvanis, the family's wealth had all gone towards defending the little kingdom from the Kaljuk invaders during the destructive three-year war.

"But wasn't everything lost in the war?" she murmured stupidly.

"The family holdings in Parvan were turned over to the royal house for the war effort," he informed her. "Much was destroyed. Jamshid had the foresight not to leave you any of the Parvan property, however, and I assure you that your inheritance, and your son's, is virtually intact."

And your son's. "Oh."

"Except for one thing. We thought that perhaps, on discovering your pregnancy, he might have entrusted it to you. Did Jamshid ever give you a jewel, Rosalind?"

"What, you mean a ring? He gave me a gold wedding band. We were in such a hurry before he went home…"

"Not a gold band. A very large diamond ring—or perhaps, the key to a safety deposit box?"

She shook her head, mystified. Again, he could not

be sure of her. "A very large diamond? Larger than *this?*"

"It is a family heirloom that belonged to Jamshid but was not among his effects when he died. He would have wanted his son to have it."

"His son," she murmured.

"The family is naturally very eager to meet you and the boy. We would like to ask you, Rosalind, to visit—"

Rosalind looked down at her hands in her lap, watching the ring with deep sadness, and thought how different her life might have been.

"I'm sorry," she said, interrupting him with quiet firmness. "Jamshid had no son. The day after I got that—that letter from your grandfather, I had a miscarriage. I lost Jamshid's baby."

Three

There was a startled silence. "A miscarriage?" he repeated softly. He did not look towards the entrance, where the plastic dinosaur was just visible.

She remembered the terrible, stabbing pain as she read the letter, as if the old man had taken a knife to her womb. As if her child had responded to such viciousness by refusing to be born into the world.

"It was the letter," she murmured. "I knew it was the letter. It's why I've hated you all so much."

He sat in silence, staring at her with a mixture of doubt and sadness. But there was nothing more to say. Rosalind shook her head, made a slight shrugging movement, then got up. She went to the bathroom, rinsed her face in cold water, stared at the ring, gazed at her reflection for a minute in blank disbelief, and came back.

He was sitting where she had left him, holding one

of the glass ornaments from the table, absently watching the snow settle around a perfect red rose. He looked up as she crossed the room and stopped in front of him.

"I'm going to make some coffee. Would you like some?"

"Thank you."

Moving around the kitchen, getting down the *cafetière,* filling the kettle, laying the tray, she could see him through the doorway. He sat on the sofa in the kind of coiled relaxation that could leap into action very quickly. He absently shook the ornament again, and a cloud of snow bubbled up and hid the rose.

"How did you meet Jamshid? Were you a student, too?"

She shook her head. "Not at the same time he was. I'd already done an undergrad degree in Parvani, and was working at the Embassy of Parvan as a junior translator. I was mostly doing stuff for tourist publications. Prince Kavian and Arash and Jamshid came and were living upstairs at the embassy," she explained.

"I was studying in Paris for much of that time. But my sister was a student at the university here at the same time as Jamshid," he remarked. She was measuring the coffee, and looked up as he spoke. "Do you remember a girl named Lamis al Azzam?"

The little scoop caught the edge of the glass *cafetière* and leapt from her grasp, the fine-ground coffee spraying all over the counter. Rosalind muttered and reached for a sponge.

Next thing she knew, he was in the doorway, still holding the rose ornament. With forced calm, Rosalind wiped up the spilled grounds, dusted the residue from her pale blue shirt, rinsed her hands and the sponge under the tap.

As she carefully measured another scoop of coffee into the *cafetière,* she said, "I knew Lamis, yes." How much would Lamis have told him? "She's your sister?" she repeated, carefully wiping all expression from her voice.

He nodded. Rosalind swallowed. This was a complication she didn't need. She would have to be careful. She lifted the kettle and poured boiling water over the grounds. The scent of coffee rose strong in the air.

"Why don't you have the same name?"

He waved his hand as if the answer would entail some obscure cultural explanation that wasn't worth the trouble.

"You must be from Barakat, then? Jamshid told me once that other branches of the family were in Bagestan and the Barakat Emirates."

He hesitated. "Yes. We are in Barakat. My mother was half sister to Jamshid's father. But the family is Bagestani originally."

She wondered if he had mentioned Lamis as a way of gaining her trust. If so, it was having the opposite effect. She would have to be on her guard with him.

She lifted the tray, and he backed out of the doorway to let her pass. She carried it into the sitting room and set it on the low black table as they sat again.

"Jamshid was from Bagestan originally? He never told me that." She poured coffee into the delicate cream-coloured porcelain cup, set a spoon in the saucer and passed it to him.

"He was born there," Najib said briefly. He noted the hesitation that had crept into her manner. So she did know something. The mention of Bagestan had made her wary. He stirred sugar into his cup, laid the little spoon on his saucer, accepted a sweet biscuit from the plate she offered.

"Really! And what made the family leave?" she asked, in a light, false voice.

Overdoing the ingenuousness, he advised her silently.

"Lamis is married now, with a young child. She works in television in Barakat." He lifted the little rose again. "She collects ornaments like this."

A fact Rosalind knew well. The ornament was not in the same style as the others on her table. The others were mostly her own choice, a carved jade figurine, a chunk of raw amethyst, a polished rose crystal set in an antique wooden tripod, a decorated egg, but... *Think of me when you look at the rose, Rosalind.*

"I am on a permanent commission to buy her a new one every time I come to Europe." She was hiding something, that much was obvious. *You rushed her,* he told himself. *Relax. Let her tell you in her own time.*

She gazed for a moment at the perfect red rose, with its little translucent drop like a tear on one petal. Rosalind had never really liked the idea of the rose being imprisoned. Like a woman in purdah. It was natural to think of Lamis when she looked at the rose: Lamis *was* the rose.

"My sister was not the same woman when she returned from her time in England," Najib murmured. "Do you know what happened while she was here to change her?"

The black gaze seemed to probe her. Rosalind dropped her eyes and nervously adjusted one of the other ornaments on the table, then forced herself to meet his gaze again. She shrugged. "What, for example?"

"I never knew. She never spoke of it. But she had been a carefree young woman. She came home marked by...suffering." He set down the glass ball with a kind of protective care, as if the rose, or the thought of his sister, called up an instinctive tenderness for anything weaker than himself.

Rosalind felt almost hypnotized by the gentle voice, the dark, dark eyes, the strong, sensitive hands. He sounded like a man in touch with life. It would be a relief to confide in him, but... The corners of her mouth pulled down to signal ignorance, she shook her head.

"Maybe it was because of the war," she said.

But he only shook his head in his turn, still watching her, and somehow Rosalind felt compelled to speak.

"We heard a rumour that Lamis went home under a bit of a cloud," she offered, a little desperately. "Gambling, or something. They said she lost an absolute bundle in some Mayfair casino and her family had to bail her out."

"That was true." He sipped his coffee. "But such a thing as this could not have caused the change I am speaking of." His eyes were on her again, as if he knew she knew.

"But you were here yourself. Surely you would have known if anything happened?"

"I went home, like Jamshid, just before the Kaljuk War. Lamis remained to complete her studies."

She said, "Did Lamis ever mention me?"

"She never talked about her time here. Did she know of your marriage?"

Rosalind shrugged, not sure what to say. "People generally did," she temporized.

He nodded, drained his coffee cup, set it down.

"Well, it is no surprise if she was afraid to tell my grandfather. The messenger's fate is well-known. Perhaps you will enjoy making her acquaintance again."

"Oh, sure!" Rosalind smiled to hide her racing thoughts, her quickened heartbeat. "When is she coming to England?"

He frowned at her.

"Do you have no intention of visiting East Barakat to inspect your inheritance and meet the family, Rosalind?"

Once she had dreamed of such a trip. But that was long ago.

Rosalind hesitated. "I don't know," she began. She glanced at her watch and leapt in sheer horror when she realized what time it was.

"Oh!" she cried, slamming down her cup so that it rattled. "I'm sorry, I completely forgot! I—have an appointment." She jumped to her feet. "You'll have to excuse me, I'm very late."

He obediently slipped the papers back into his case, snapped it shut and got to his feet. He followed her to the door. She was practically running.

"Goodbye," she said quickly.

"We will talk again," he said.

"Yes," she babbled. "Yes, give me a call...."

She opened the door, but he did not step through. Instead, Najib al Makhtoum bent to set down his case beside the cheerful plastic dinosaur on wheels. He straightened, and Rosalind's breath caught in her throat as his hands grasped her shoulders.

He stared down into her face. For a strange moment,

his mouth above hers, they seemed to slip into some other reality, a reality where they knew each other very well, where he had the right to kiss her. Rosalind had the crazy thought that by putting the ring on her finger he had opened a door onto another life, and tendrils of that other possibility were now reaching for them. His black gaze pierced her, searching for her soul, and her lips parted involuntarily.

They blinked, and the world shook itself back into place. *She is a complete temptress,* he told himself. *You will have to be on your guard every moment.* Jamshid's behaviour was a mystery no longer. His judgement must have been derailed as powerfully as if he were drugged.

"Rosalind, this is of immense importance," he said. "You cannot guess how vital it is that you tell me the truth. Do not allow an old grievance to affect you any further. Did you give birth to Jamshid's son?"

His long fingers were painful on the soft flesh at her shoulders. The look in his eyes frightened her.

"Why is it so important?"

"I am not at liberty to explain. But I ask you to believe that it is."

It was her pain speaking when she said, "How can a possibility that was totally rejected five years ago suddenly become a matter of immense importance?"

He shook her. "Tell me."

She pulled out of his grasp and turned away. "I have told you. Jamshid's baby died," she said, her voice raw. She looked at her watch again. "Please go. I'm late."

"Goodbye, Rosalind," he said, picking up his case. "I'll be in touch."

He strode down the corridor to the wrought-iron

cage that held the elegant Art Deco lift. But before he could push the button, it clanged and heaved and started its upward journey from the lobby.

Rosalind bit her lip. Instead of closing the door she stood there, nervously planted in the doorway, following the sound of the machine's tortured progress. How could she have failed to think of this?

Najib glanced at her, his eyes widening and then narrowing into alertness at what he saw in her face.

Rosalind waited with a kind of fatalistic foreknowledge as the lift creaked up three floors and ground to a stop. Then the door opened and, as she had known they would, a small, excited boy and a pretty teenage girl stepped out.

Najib, holding the door open with one arm, turned to watch in disbelief as the child shot down the hall towards Rosalind, a decorated sheet of blue construction paper clutched in one tiny hand. Rosalind knelt down and held her arms open.

"Mommy, Mommy!" cried Sam, his eyes glowing, as he flung himself into her embrace. "Look what I made you!"

Over his head, Rosalind saw Najib al Makhtoum's dark, accusing gaze rake over her for one horrible moment. Then he turned and stepped into the lift.

"He's the living spit of the old man," said Naj.

"Damn," came Ashraf's fervent voice. "Damn, damn, damn."

The was a silence. "And she knows nothing about the Rose?"

"So she said. But she is living in a place she certainly did not buy on a translator's income. In Kensington."

Ashraf cursed again. "You think she sold the Rose? Who to?"

Naj shook his head, his lips pursed. "No guesses there. Depends how much she knew."

"She knows enough to deny the kid is Jamshid's."

"And maybe when she's had a little time to absorb the facts she'll stop denying it. She naturally assumed we all knew about the exchange of letters and left her to swing in the breeze. And God knows what she thought Jamshid's motives were."

"Naj, if he gave her the Rose she can't have doubted his sincerity."

"True. Well, maybe she sold it because Grandfather's letter killed off any sense of loyalty."

"It's not fitting together," Ash said.

"She'll tell me eventually," Naj said, though he wondered whether it would be himself who cracked. "It may take her time to get up the courage to confess."

"We don't have that luxury, time," Ashraf pointed out. "We have to bring the boy here, and we have to do it yesterday."

"I know."

"Can you handle it, Naj? Want any backup?"

He thought of her eyes in that odd, fleeting moment when life had seemed different. There had been a promise there, of a kind he had been waiting for all his life without realizing it.

"I'll handle it," he said.

Sam and Rosie sat on the sofa, Rosie cuddling her son as she read him a story from a book they had chosen from the library and he told her about the pictures. It was something they did nearly every day.

But he was making do with less than her full attention today. Rosalind stroked her son's head, kissed his hair, and murmured approvingly as he talked, but her eyes kept dropping to the beautiful ring, and her mind kept slipping back to her meeting with Najib al Makhtoum.

Her head was buzzing with questions. Why had Jamshid never told his grandfather about the marriage? Why had he not told her he was from such a rich family? Had they really only found the will recently, or did the family have some reason for suddenly being willing to part with her inheritance?

If so, that reason centred in the possibility that Jamshid had an heir. He had spoken about a jewel, but how likely was it that they really believed Jamshid would have given her anything so valuable? She looked at the diamond Najib had put on her finger. She knew little about precious stones, but this one had to be two carats at least. Bigger than this one—what were they talking about? The Koh-i-Noor? Why would Jamshid have given it to her when he hadn't even told her about his wealthy background?

He had given her gifts, of course. But nothing more valuable than an ordinary man would give his fiancée. He had bought her a leather jacket she had admired, and given her a gold chain with a heart on her birthday. Rosalind's eyes drifted down to the coffee table. And the little antique crystal ornament when she told him she thought she was pregnant. That was absolutely all.

She stared at the diamond ring Najib had just given her. She still could hardly believe it. Was it even real? But the light caught it as she moved her hand, and her

question was answered. There was unmistakable fire
in the heart of the stone.

Someone somewhere was very disturbed, that much
was clear. Najib al Makhtoum had come, not so much
to right an old wrong, not to see that she got her inheritance after five years, but to discover if Jamshid
had a son.

She wondered if Najib had asked his sister about
her. But anything Lamis might have told him was now
overshadowed by the fact that he had seen Sam. He
would be back, of course. She would have to plan
what to say to him when he came.

Four

"Hello again, Rosalind."

Rosalind tilted her head in a small nod, marvelling at how strong the family likeness was, especially around the eyes. They were Sam's eyes.

"Najib. You do have a knack with the security guard. What is it, a Cloak of Invisibility?"

He gave her a look. "May I come in?"

"Do you think you might have phoned first?"

"Would you have been here if I had done so?" he asked dryly.

She lifted a cool eyebrow to let him know what she thought of that. "What do you want at this hour on a Sunday?"

Najib looked at Rosalind without answering. Her bare legs seemed too long under the unbleached cotton of her shirt, her hair was tousled, her lips vulnerable without any makeup, her eyes slightly swollen, and with a blow that rocked him he understood clearly that the answer to that was, *I want you.*

He clenched his jaw, because he almost spoke the words on the thought. Instead he said urgently, ''Let me in. I have to tell you—''

She moved to block the doorway. ''How did you get past the doorman, and this time I want to know?''

He glared at her. Her distrust of him suddenly infuriated him. ''I got in because I am officially a resident of this building. I have bought an apartment here,'' he explained with irritated emphasis.

She goggled at him. ''You—you *what?* I don't believe you!''

''Money can do many things. You know it, so what is there to surprise you? Now let me in.''

He put his hand on her arm, and that was a mistake. His skin seemed to glue itself to hers. Impelled by the urgency in his eyes, the heat of his flesh, she stepped back, and he followed her inside, his foot pushing the door shut behind him.

Electricity from his touch rushed along her arm and through her body. What a fool she was not to have recognized this attraction for what it was before! But it had needed this combination of morning, being taken by surprise, and a sense of her own vulnerability, apparently, to show her what should have been totally obvious: it had a potency that was frightening.

And just her luck she couldn't even trust him.

She glared down at his hand, strong on her bare flesh, and wished it were her fate to give in to such strength, to be protected by it instead of threatened. ''Let go of me,'' she said hoarsely.

He was standing close, too close. Another mistake. He could smell the perfume of her skin, and worse, he could smell bed on her mussed hair, the drowsy smell of a woman newly climbed from the sheets.

"Let go," she said again, her voice weaker, barely a whisper.

He willed his hand to lift from her warmth, but it only tightened on her. With almost overwhelming urgency, he wanted to pick her up and carry her back to her bed, undress her, make love to her, make her his before she could decide against him. His body leapt with the hungry need to lose himself in her.

"I am sorry," he said.

He lifted his free hand to her cheek, slipping his fingers under the fall of her hair to cup her head, and bent his head to the dangerous, inevitable kiss.

In a sudden burst of paranoia, Rosalind thought, *He's trying to use sex as a weapon.* She stepped back abruptly, breaking his hold, and his lips touched only air. And the same pang of regret pierced them both.

"What are you here for?" she demanded coldly.

He abruptly lost patience.

"I have seen your son, Rosalind. Why have you lied to me about so grave a matter?" he demanded fiercely.

As the dark eyes burned accusingly into hers, Rosalind felt the hairs lift all over her body. "I have not lied to you!" she snapped. "And what is grave about it?" She was beginning to wish she had never told him the truth. What harm would it do to let the family believe that Jamshid had left an heir?

"Shall we sit down?" he said grimly.

"I am not going to have this conversation with you now!" Rosalind cried. For answer he simply strode over to the sofa and set his briefcase on the table. Weakly, she followed him, demanding, "Why didn't you phone?"

"Sit down, Rosalind," he commanded softly, and to her own fury she could not resist the authority in his voice.

She sat and crossed her legs, shifting uncomfortably. The thick, woven cotton shirt she used as a bathrobe was longer than lots of dresses, but she felt naked as he sat beside her.

Rosalind opened her mouth to say she was going to get dressed first, but Najib bent forward and clicked his briefcase ominously open, and the sounds of the locks were like neat little bullets into her spine, paralysing her.

He drew out a long, narrow piece of buff paper, a printed form neatly inscribed in black ballpoint, straightened and held it in front of her.

Certified Copy of an Entry of Birth, she read, and though she knew exactly what it was, her eye automatically glanced over the particulars. *Name—Samir Jawad... Sex—Male...*

She looked up into the eyes that were gravely watching her.

"Well?" she said.

"In the summer you were pregnant with Jamshid's child. The following spring you gave birth."

"Did I?" It was ridiculous to expect him to believe her word against this, but she was angry with him nevertheless.

A long, well-shaped forefinger ruthlessly underlined a column as he looked at her. *"Mother—Rosalind Olivia Lewis,"* he read.

Rosalind heaved a breath and tried to get control. "This is not going to get you anywhere," she told him. "I—"

"Father—Jamshid Bahrami."

"What do you want?" she demanded in exasperated tones. "What do you care? It's been five years! What do you care whether my son inherits Jamshid's property or not?"

Najib turned his head sideways to look at her. He did not answer, and she felt a shiver of real alarm. *So grave a matter,* he had said. But how grave could money be? If a will and an unknown heir are belatedly found, that might be very inconvenient to some, but grave?

Why had the discovery that Jamshid had a wife brought his cousin all this way in person? The question was obvious and she should have seen it before. Why hadn't they just sent her a solicitor's letter informing her of the inheritance, asking if there was a child? Why did they care so desperately about it?

"Look. Sam is—" she began, but broke off with a gasp when Najib al Makhtoum released the birth certificate and grasped her wrist.

"Do not *lie* to me, Rosalind!"

The paper floated in graceful swoops to the floor. They were still for an electric moment of staring into each other's eyes, and again were disturbed by the nearness of that other potential behind the moment. Then Rosalind tore her hand out of his grip and stood up. Whatever thoughts she had entertained about maybe giving in were lost in her fury.

"Don't accuse me of lying! You know nothing about my life!"

"I know that you registered this birth," he said, picking up the birth certificate from the floor and dropping it into his briefcase before getting to his feet. "In doing so you swore that Jamshid was the father of your son. Now you tell me otherwise. Which of your statements am I not to say was a lie, Rosalind?''

He had a powerful aura, and she felt overwhelmed. She strode away, into the dining area, crossed her arms and stood looking out at the grey, damp street. A Bentley cruised by below in silent luxury.

''In this country a woman's husband is deemed to be the father of her children,'' she said, ''whether he is the biological father or not. Jamshid is not Sam's biological father.''

He followed her to the window, his mouth tight.

''You were pregnant and you gave birth to a child, Rosalind. There was no miscarriage. True or false?''

She glared at him.

''Either you lied to Jamshid and my grandfather five years ago, or you are lying to me now. There is no other possibility.''

There was another possibility, but she could not tell him what it was. She had to forcefully resist the crazy impulse that said it would be safe to tell him the truth. Najib was the last person she could tell, and what a stupid twist of fate it was that it should be he who had come here.

''You know nothing!'' she exploded harshly.

''A woman does not have a miscarriage and then give birth a few months later,'' he said remorselessly. ''Tell me the truth!''

What was it all about? Rosie's skin began to creep with a dread of the unknown. There was much more here than she knew. Thank God she had not just taken the easy way out. Whatever this was, she had to keep Sam out of it.

''I have told you the truth. I am not going to repeat myself,'' she said stonily.

"Why did you not put his father's name on the birth certificate, then?" He did not pause for an answer. "Jamshid is the father. That is why you put his name on the birth certificate. You did not lie to my grandfather. You are lying now, and it is a foolish, dangerous lie."

"You know *nothing* about *anything* in my life," she said with angry emphasis, her hands clenching on air. Furious with him, and yet knowing that there was nothing else for him to think.

"Shall I believe that my grandfather was justified in the words he used to you in his letter, after all, Rosalind? Shall I believe that, not certain who had fathered your child, you chose to trick Jamshid into marriage?"

Rosalind straightened, head back, staring at him, her mouth tight with fury. Her hand lifted of its own accord, and she slapped him across the cheek with a violence fuelled by five long years of bitter hurt.

His eyes blackened as if this ignited feeling he had been keeping under precarious control. His hands closed roughly on her upper arms and he grabbed her close to ram his face down into hers. "Do not use violence with me!" he warned.

There was silence as they stared into each other's eyes from point-blank range. She watched in almost detached fascination the angry quiver of the thick black lashes, the expansion of his pupils, the flame of danger. She counted the pounding of her blood in her temples, heard the little ragged pants of her breathing. As if from a distance she realized that Najib al Makhtoum was not a man to cross.

They both surfaced from the trance. He dropped his hands from her. Each turned away. Rosalind crossed her arms over her breasts, her hands involuntarily massaging her upper arms where he had gripped her.

"Get out," she said.

"He is the living image of my grandfather," Najib said, behind her. "I am sorry. I accuse you of nothing except being bitterly hurt and too angry to forgive. But this must be put aside for the sake of the boy. The res—"

"Get out of my house and get out of my life!"

Najib gave an indignant half laugh as the strange, soft possibility of deeper communication between them evaporated.

"I cannot do that," he said, and at his tone chills raced up her spine.

"Why?"

"You force my hand, and no doubt you will spend many hours regretting it. Rosalind, your son is in danger. He must go into hiding for a period. Only in this way can we protect him effectively."

"Danger?" She felt as though he had smashed the side of her head, sending all coherent thought flying. "Danger from what?"

"People who will wish harm to Jamshid's son when they learn of his existence."

Oh, this was much worse than she had guessed a moment ago. Rosie almost sobbed. "He is not Jamshid's son! Why won't you believe me?"

"Because the family resemblance is unmistakable. And because he was registered as Jamshid's son. Even if I could believe you, there are others who will not."

Hot and then cold raced over her skin. "Who are these people? Who will tell them that Sam is Jamshid's son?"

"No one will tell them. But it will not be long before they learn."

"Because you've led them to me!" she accused hotly.

He shook his head. "No."

"Why have you stirred this up? No one would have known about me or Sam if you—"

He shook his head again, and overrode her. "It was easy for me to find this information. It is lying everywhere on the ground, like nuts under a tree! Others will find it no more difficult."

She interrupted harshly, "It's been lying there for the past five years. Why is it only interesting now?"

"This is precisely what cannot be explained to you."

"Why would they want to hurt a son of Jamshid's?" Fear seemed to wash over her in waves. "Who are you? Who are your enemies?"

"I have already told you more than is good for you to know," said al Makhtoum.

"Is it just Jamshid's son, or is the whole family at risk? Your children, for example—are they in danger, too?"

"I am not married. But your son is by no means alone in the danger."

Rosalind whispered faintly, "Is it a feud or something?"

"I can say no more, Rosalind. In a little while you will learn more. But I tell you that you can trust me, and you must. Time is short."

She eyed him, chewing her lip. "And if I trusted you, what would I do?"

"You would accompany me to East Barakat, where we can protect you and your son effectively."

"East Barakat." She licked her lips. "For how long?"

He hesitated. "A few weeks—two or three months."

"Three months?" she repeated in surprise. "And what then?"

"I am not at liberty to explain to you now how the situation is likely to change. But it will change."

"And after that—Sam and I will be able to go back to our ordinary lives?"

He glanced away, looked back and met her eyes again. "I hope so. I believe so. If we are successful."

She said furiously, "You *hope* so?"

"The fault, if there is one, is not mine. Jamshid had no right to marry you as he did. Whatever happens next, your part in it was inevitable from the moment that he did so."

"What—" she began, but he overrode her.

"Rosalind," Najib said, with an urgency that silenced her. "I assure you that you can trust me. Jamshid would wish you to obey me in this."

She was terrified. She had no idea which way to turn. Should she trust or fear him? It had to be one or the other. There was no middle ground. But her brain lay kicking feebly, unable to function.

"Mommy?"

The questioning voice came from behind them, and they both whirled. Sam, tousled with sleep, sweet as a Victorian painting, stood at the doorway of his room. From one hand dangled his toy lamb.

"Good morning, darling," Rosalind said brightly.

His wide eyes watching Najib with wary curiosity, he came to her side, grabbed her thigh, and continued to stare up at the stranger.

To her surprise, Najib squatted down, to be on a level with him.

"Hi," he said. Sam watched the stranger for a long, grave moment, then glanced uncertainly up into his mother's face.

"Sam, this is Najib," she said.

Sam looked at him again, considering. Najib waited, allowing himself to be scrutinized.

"Hi," Sam said at last. Then he pulled up his lamb. "This is Lambo," he said. Rosalind caught her breath. He never introduced his favourite stuffed animal except to people he had decided to trust.

Najib nodded, taking it as seriously as the boy meant it. He reached out and shook a hoof. "Hi," he said again.

Najib put out his hand, and when the child, as if entranced, moved out from behind his mother's leg and reached a trusting hand towards him, he clasped it with the strong, comforting masculine protectiveness that Rosalind recognized as what drew her, against her will.

And as if hypnotized by the promise of safety and by the dark eyes so like his own, Sam stepped into the circle of Najib al Makhtoum's arm, looking up with a yearning that pulled at Rosalind's heart, for in that trusting gaze was reflected the need for the thing that she, with all her caring, could never give him: a father's love.

"Are you my friend?" he asked.

"Yes, I'm your friend," Najib said, without hesitation. "I'm your very good friend."

Encouraged by this, Sam pursued, "Are you my father?"

"Sam…" Rosalind began in embarrassment. But Najib didn't seem at all put out by the question.

"I don't know," he said. When Sam's eyes widened, for Najib was the first man who had not answered this question with a quick, embarrassed no, he explained, "God's will works in lots of different ways. But I do know I'm going to look after you for the next little while just the way your own father would have wanted me to. Okay?"

Sam blinked, not quite understanding it all, but getting the intention all right, Rosalind saw. "Okay," he said soberly, nodding as if they were fixing a pact.

"What *do* you think you're telling him?" Rosalind muttered, trying for a tone that would convey to Najib al Makhtoum exactly what she meant without scaring Sam.

He glanced up. "The truth," he said dryly.

"You know perfectly well that—" she began, then, as Sam looked at her uncertainly, relaxed her tone "—the relationship he has enquired about does not exist between you and never will. And as for looking after—"

Najib laughed, with such genuine humour that Sam broke into a huge grin and giggled with him. He hugged the boy and got to his feet.

"Rosalind, do you tell me that life has not yet taught you how God plays with the designs of mortals? Do you not fear to tempt fate with such extreme declarations of your intentions?"

"And how exactly would God go about turning you into Sam's father?" she demanded.

He eyed her with a warmth that made her cheeks hot. "We might get married," he observed.

Rosalind's skin twitched all down her spine. She felt

how dangerous this conversation was, for the yearning
that his words raised in her. How often she had wished
there were someone to share the joys and cares of
Sam's upbringing with her. "And how do you know
what his father would want?" she went on, as if she
hadn't heard that.

"I know that any father wants his child protected,"
Najib said. "But Jamshid in particular, whose father
was—died when he was an infant, would wish for me
to love and cherish his own son as he could not."

It seemed as if every time he opened his mouth, he
said three different things she needed to challenge, and
in the attempt to decide which to attack first, she lost
the chance to challenge any.

Sam was looking up anxiously, as if he was beginning to sense her hostility, and Rosalind bent down.
"I need to talk with Najib for a little bit, Sam. Would
you like to go back to bed and read Lambo a story?
And then you can have your shower."

When Sam agreed to this she took him back to his
bedroom and settled him on his pillows with a cloth
picture book, his lamb in the crook of one arm.

"Rosalind," Najib al Makhtoum said on her return
to the kitchen. "Please allow me to make arrange-
ments for your protection, and your son's. Time may
be shorter even than we suspect."

His words frightened her, not least because she was
torn. And it seemed that the part that wanted to believe
she could trust him was getting stronger. That meant
she had to be on guard not just against him, but against
her own instincts.

When she hesitated, Najib said, "Rosalind, do not
risk his happiness, or your own. Let me look after you
both."

"What will you arrange?" she asked.

"Do you have passports?"

"Sam is on my passport," she said firmly. Her son was going nowhere without her.

"Then I will arrange to fly you to East Barakat immediately. How soon can you be ready? Tomorrow?"

She felt panic creeping through her at the speed at which he moved. "Next Saturday," she hazarded.

He frowned and shook his head once. "A week is too long. We must leave by Wednesday, Thursday at the latest."

"Friday," Rosalind said. "I can't be ready before Friday," because some distant voice told her she would need thinking time.

Five

Rosie paced her apartment after he had gone, watching the sun spread into the morning sky.

Your son is in danger. He must go into hiding.

The words ricocheted around in her head. She had no way of knowing whether it was true, or a lie designed to frighten her into acquiescence. But she couldn't afford to ignore the warning. Either she trusted Najib, or she got out of town under her own steam. She had to protect Sam, because Najib was right in one thing—anyone who was interested would come to the conclusion that Sam was Jamshid's son.

Why would a son of Jamshid's be in danger? Some family feud? Some ancient tribal thing? She had heard of tribes taking vengeance against each other, one death and then another, down through the generations, but it seemed so improbable in the modern world.

Jamshid had no right to marry you....

Why? Why hadn't Jamshid told his grandfather about their marriage? She remembered the letters he had written to her five years ago, before he went to fight. He had told her that the family was delighted with his news.

His grandfather's letter had proved that, far from delighted, they had been ignorant of her existence, and from that moment Rosalind had doubted everything. But Jamshid had always been optimistic. No doubt he had planned to get it all sorted out before bringing his wife home.

And now they did know, or thought they did, and instead of happy, they were paranoid.

Shivers chased up and down her back. It was like being surrounded by animals in the dark. All she could see was the firelight reflected in a dozen pairs of eyes.

It did not help that when he tried to kiss her she had discovered how attracted she was. Well, he was a deeply attractive man, if too rugged to be conventionally handsome. And he also looked like a man you could lean on—so long as he was on your side.

The trouble was that the central relationship of her life was with her son. Rosalind dated, she had friends, but there was no one in whom she fully confided, no one on whom she felt she could lean emotionally in a troubled moment. Her secret had isolated her, without her ever meaning that it should.

Or perhaps it was just that, after Jamshid, she had been wary of trusting anyone.

However much she distrusted him, though, she sensed in Najib al Makhtoum a masculine strength that had been absent from her life for too long. She had been strong for five years, and now she realized how tired she was.

She could not risk leaning on Najib. But, trust him or not, she had to operate on the assumption that he was telling the truth when he said Sam was in danger.

She couldn't afford to ignore that. Even if she couldn't be certain it wasn't Najib himself who was the threat.

"Yeah. She agreed. But unless I'm very mistaken, she will now be having serious second thoughts."

An involuntary yawn overcame him, and Najib rubbed his scalp with quick vigorous fingers, causing his short, thick hair, already tousled with sleep, to stand in spikes. Outside the window, a blackbird was singing of summer with full-throated ease. Sunrise slanted in from the east, illuminating his crumpled white pyjama bottoms and naked feet. Under the open bathrobe his chest was bare. His body, stretching out from his chair, was supported on sharply angled legs, firmly planted feet. His toes dug into the silk carpet, caressing the luxurious pile in absent sensual appreciation.

"Which means what?"

Ashraf did have a way of forgetting the time difference, Najib reflected. But he felt no complaint. During the Kaljuk War he had acquired the ability to wake and sleep at will, and it still stood him in good stead when doing business across the world's time lines.

"Well, my guess is, she'll do a runner."

There was silence as that sank in. "Ripe pickings for the opposition, in fact," Ashraf muttered.

"Maybe." Najib swung his bathrobe belt with his free hand. He was more annoyed with himself than he could remember ever being. He had practically jumped her. No wonder if she was afraid to trust him.

He wanted her to trust him, to tell him. Najib thrust himself to his feet, the phone still at his ear, and wandered over to the desk in a far corner of the room, between two huge sash windows, both open onto the morning breeze. He stood for a moment looking down at the rich green of the world-famous park below. A rider went by on a high-spirited grey.

"Do you think he's already got to her?" Ashraf asked.

Najib frowned. He did not want to believe her capable of that. "My guess is, no."

Rosalind's five-year-old photo lay face up on the desk, the early sun bathing it in rich pink and gold. Leaning against the window, the phone under his ear, he reached for it and dropped his eyes to the smiling, trusting face of a girl who had feared nothing.

Ashraf answered with another question. "Then why is she lying?"

"It might be just because she sold the Rose."

She did not look at *him* like this. Cool suspicious mockery was the expression he saw, and he was aware of a deep irritation that it should be so.

"That doesn't cover why she's lying about the boy."

What kind of fool was he? There was no reason on earth for her to look at him with this expression, and no good reason for him to want her to. Except for the strange sensation that rose up in him, telling him that he should have met her in other circumstances, that a different relationship would have been possible between them....

She had entered his dreams last night, and in his dreams she had trusted him.

"Is it possible Jamshid told her everything and she wants no part of it?" Ash suggested.

"Then she would have known why I was there, wouldn't she?"

He gazed at the face. She was hiding something, he knew it. But what, and how dangerous was the information? "I'd like to tell her the truth, Ash. I think if she knew…"

Ashraf snorted. "You just finished telling me she hates us all. If you tell her the truth and she goes to—we've been over that, Naj."

Najib nodded absently. They had discussed it from every angle, and Ash was right: it was a risk they couldn't take. In the wrong hands—and with the Rose, too—Jamshid's son would be an unbeatable weapon.

"Is there any chance, any chance at all, that she is telling the truth and this isn't Jamshid's son?" Ashraf prodded.

"It's on the birth cert—" Naj began, but Ashraf interrupted.

"She might have lied from the start."

That would mean she had cheated on Jamshid, lied to him about it…then lied to his grandfather in the letter, and all probably for no worthier motive than money. Naj stared at the photo. *Women have cheated men going to war before this, haven't they?* he reminded himself cynically. *And you don't exactly have a history of recognizing when a woman is taking you for a ride.*

He didn't want to believe that this face was capable of that kind of dishonesty.

"If that were the case, why would she deny it now, when it's finally payoff time?"

Maybe it was just the sense of waste that consumed

him. The waste of such loving trust, destroyed by a
letter from his grandfather so viciously cruel it had
poisoned the whole family's reputation. Could he ever
make her understand how history had destroyed a
once-great man, made him prey to suspicion and con-
tempt for his fellow creatures?

It would be suicidally stupid to get emotionally involved with the mother of Jamshid's child at a moment
like this. They couldn't afford to have him screw up
over the next few weeks or months, whatever he did
afterwards.

Afterwards, he thought.

Providence took a hand on Monday, from a completely unexpected direction. The agency through
whom Rosalind got her freelance translation work
asked if she would be interested in a long-term assignment, translating a classical Parvani manuscript.

It sounded a lot more interesting than the trade and
technical stuff that made up the bulk of Rosie's work.
But the real excitement came when she heard the
terms: the manuscript's owner didn't want to let the
valuable book out of his possession. The job entailed
going to stay in his country house on the Cornish coast
for the time it would take her to complete the work.

It was the first time she had been offered a job like
this, though she knew such assignments were not all
that unusual. Many owners of ancient manuscripts or
collections of coins or other valuables were reluc-
tant—or forbidden by their insurance policies—to let
the treasures out of their keeping. That meant that cat-
aloguers and translators went to the treasures rather
than vice versa—sometimes to Middle Eastern pal-

aces. Assignments like that were at the top of the plum tree, and this ranked a pretty close second.

"I've got Sam," Rosie reminded her agent.

"I have explained about Sam," said Gemma. "And the response was that Sam would be welcome provided that he was a child who would obey when instructed not to play with priceless antiques. Is he?"

Rosalind reassured her, and by the time she hung up she was wearing a smile a foot wide. This required no such drastic changing of her life as she had been considering. She and Sam could simply disappear for a while and await events.

She sat back and started planning how to keep Najib al Makhtoum—or anyone else—from discovering where they had gone.

The next two days were crazy with activity. As a first step she confided to Gemma that there was someone she was avoiding, who might try to track her whereabouts.

"Oh, Rosalind! Is it a stalker?" Gemma demanded.

"I hope it's not going to come to that," Rosalind temporized, and Gemma promised not to even admit she knew Rosalind to any enquirer, until and unless she had checked with Rosalind first.

Rosalind casually mentioned a trip to North America to a neighbour and to the newsagent who delivered her morning paper. She booked and paid for tickets to New York through a neighbourhood travel agency, on a flight due to leave Thursday afternoon.

Her mail she had forwarded to a post office box. She could travel down to London every couple of weeks to pick it up without going near the apartment.

The house-sitting agency she engaged sent someone

for an interview, a responsible-looking woman with grey hair who said she understood all about plants and would keep Rosalind's in good health, was quite flexible, could start immediately and stay indefinitely if necessary.

To her, too, Rosalind told the careful lie that she was taking her son to North America. They would be travelling the continent with friends in a mobile home, and she could leave no contact number. But if Helen would take messages, Rosalind explained, she would phone once a week to get them.

So it was all in motion.

On Thursday morning, without a hitch, Rosalind turned over the keys to Helen, and she and an excited Sam climbed into the taxi en route for Victoria Station. Rosalind talked of catching the train to the airport and mentioned New York to the driver. But at Victoria, after loading a luggage trolley with their bags, she and Sam went into the ladies' room. There she tucked her hair up under a baseball cap, pulled on a pair of sunglasses and changed her jacket. She disguised Sam in a similar way and they came back out to the taxi rank.

Speaking in what she hoped would pass as an Italian accent, and pretending they had just arrived from the continent, she took a cab to Paddington, where the trains from the southwest terminated. At the station they did another quick costume change, and not long after, Rosalind and Sam had boarded their train and were heading out of London.

She was no expert, but she was pretty sure there had been no sign of a tail any part of the way.

"So she opted to run," said Ashraf.
"She opted to run," Najib agreed.

"How did she orchestrate it, just out of curiosity?"

"Agreed to come with me to East Barakat on Friday, took off on Thursday. She booked to go to New York…"

"New York?"

"But that was all dust in the eyes."

"You were pretty confident she'd do just what you wanted, weren't you?"

"There were only so many options, Ash."

Ashraf expelled a breath. "I wish she had trusted you. I'd a helluva lot rather they were both here."

"It wasn't on the cards," Naj said. "I knew it was going to be Plan B."

Six

"**M**y dear, it's very kind of you to come all this way," said Sir John, opening a door into a room that made her stop and gasp with surprised pleasure. It was a private library that looked like a movie set of a private library. Leather-bound books lined ornately worked oak shelves that ran from the floor to the very high ceilings. A movable staircase gave access to the higher shelves.

One wall held a row of massive Georgian windows facing south over a beautiful expanse of tree-sprinkled lawn and garden, backed by the deeper green of thick woods. Every foot of wall space not filled with books held the most beautiful Parvani and Bagestani paintings and artefacts she had seen outside the British Museum.

"King Kavad Panj," Rosalind murmured, as she

unconsciously moved towards a portrait that she recognized.

"Indeed," Sir John confirmed with a courtly nod. "It is one of two copies made by the artist. The other was for the palace in Parvan. His Majesty presented this one to me on my retirement, a great honour."

She had not really been surprised to learn the identity of her employer. The manuscript she was to translate had to belong to some noted collector. Sir John Cross, the former British Ambassador to Parvan, was a well-known Parvanophile, and from having served in the country for over twenty years, he had a large network of Parvani friends. They would naturally have turned to him when selling off their treasures during and after the war.

Rosalind stood gazing at the portrait, and thought with a pang how different her life would be if the Kaljuk invasion had never happened. King Kavad Panj was the father of Crown Prince Kavian, whose Cup Companion Jamshid had been. She would have seen this same portrait, but in other circumstances—in the great palace in Shahr-i Bozorg. She would almost undoubtedly have met the king. And Sir John, too, she would have met under different circumstances.

Would she have met Najib al Makhtoum? She had had a strange, indescribable feeling, both times she met him, as if she had almost known him in a different life. There was that curious phenomenon when reality flickered, as if between two different life paths....

But, of course, she reminded herself, nothing would have come of any other meeting with Najib. She would have been Jamshid's wife. So the feeling that in a different life stream they might have had the chance to be important to each other had to be wrong.

She surfaced from her reverie and found the former ambassador smiling at her. "I'm so sorry!" she exclaimed guiltily.

"Not at all, my dear. It's a pleasure to see my treasures so keenly appreciated. And do you recognize this person?" he asked, stopping in front of another royal portrait.

She frowned at another face from recent history. "I think that's the ex-Sultan of Bagestan, isn't it? Hafzuddin al Jawadi?"

"It is." He shook his head ruefully. "A great man. His overthrow was a tragedy not merely for him, but for the country. I was Her Majesty's ambassador to Bagestan during that period, as no doubt you know. My first ambassadorial posting."

Rosalind smiled apologetically. "I didn't know. I didn't study Bagestani modern history in detail. I concentrated on Parvan," she apologized.

"History," he said musingly. "I suppose it is just history now. The coup happened before you were born, of course. Nineteen sixty-nine. It doesn't seem as long ago as that. Over thirty years now of such appalling misrule. What a wonderful, civilised country it was!" He shook his head.

"A dreadful time. One felt at the mercy of very unpleasant forces—" He broke off.

Rosie frowned in surprise. "But it was just a military coup, wasn't it?"

"Well, it was and it wasn't, my dear. The coup could not have succeeded without the…complicity, shall we say, of Western oil interests. Some said it would not have been attempted without our government's strong, if covert, encouragement.

"Hafzuddin was a great democrat, you know,

within his own lights. He was a firm ally of the West, but he had a way of resisting Western hegemony. He held the unpopular conviction that self-determination was the right of every nation. He learned that not every democracy agreed with this view.''

Rosalind watched the old man, fascinated. "Do you mean the overthrow of the al Jawadis was orchestrated—''

He smiled at her, without filling in the blank, then turned back to his contemplation of the portrait.

"Of course it had been made to look like an entirely homegrown movement, but Hafzuddin was no fool. When there was no outcry from the Western democracies, when not one of the nations with whom he had been so friendly so much as murmured in protest, he understood that he had been betrayed not only by his protégé Ghasib, who owed him everything, but also by his declared friends among Western governments, including, I am sorry to say it, our own.''

His inside knowledge of the area left her openmouthed, and Rosie listened in fascination to the insights he had about the history and art of Parvan and its neighbours.

"Now, my dear," Sir John said later, when he had showed her the manuscript she was here to translate and she was settling down to work, "I hope you won't feel you have to hurry. *Irfani Arifan* has waited over five hundred years for a translator, and a few weeks here or there will make no difference. I shall enjoy having your company about the place.''

Sam was in heaven. There were acres of walled land around the broad expanse of lawn that surrounded the house, filled with streams and thick woods and enough secret places to delight any child. The housekeeper had two young daughters who were very happy to have a new, younger playmate to show it all to. He disappeared with them each morning and returned for lunch dirty, wet and happy, with tales of rabbits chased, foxes sighted, butterflies, frogs, and fish in endless profusion, before eating with a better appetite than Rosalind had ever seen in him and then rushing off again.

One day, having seen Sam and the girls off on another adventure, Rosalind paused for a moment on the broad terrace to take in the glorious morning, and noticed a man in the distance, in the typical country Wellington boots, Barbour jacket, hat, and shotgun, striding across the lawn after them. She thought nothing of it until the next morning, when the same thing happened. And the next.

"Are the children being watched?" she asked Sir John that evening.

Sir John was reaching for his wineglass, but at her abrupt change of subject he turned his head. The glass went over, spreading red on the spotless white damask. He waited in silence as the butler attended to it and refilled his glass.

"Ah, you've seen Jenkins, I expect," he said with an apologetic twitch of his mouth. "My head groundskeeper. Not a fan of letting children run wild over the place, I'm afraid. He cultivates various wild species in the wood and he would rather the children were restricted to the lawns. Very jealous of his territory. He won't frighten them—he simply makes sure they aren't heading for any vulnerable plantations."

This didn't quite put to rest her feeling of disquiet. "Has he been in your employ long?" Rosalind asked.

He looked startled. "Oh—oh yes, my dear! All his life. I knew his grandfather very well. They—uh, the family lost their estate. Oh, you have nothing to worry about with Jenkins. Quite the right sort. He'll see the children come to no harm."

Most evenings she had dinner with her host after Sam was in bed. He was a very cultured and educated man, and as well as an enormous interest and learning in Parvan and Bagestan culture and art, he was also fascinating to listen to on the subject of his local area, which was rich in early British archaeological remains. He told her about several prehistoric sites within a half hour's drive, including a stone circle, which Rosalind immediately decided to visit at the first opportunity.

"Perhaps you know we have a rather splendid specimen of a prehistoric standing stone on the property itself," he told her early in her visit. She had wandered around since, half looking for it, but without success.

"I haven't found your standing stone," she said one night over dinner.

"Well, it isn't always easy to find," he said, his eyes twinkling as he drank his wine. "But it is a tradition of the stone that people must find it for themselves. Some people stumble upon it almost instantly, but most find it rather difficult. And there are one or two who have never found it. I can tell you, as I tell all my guests who are interested, that it lies in the woods in the southwest quadrant of the property. But beyond that, my dear, it's up to you."

She couldn't get Najib al Makhtoum out of her mind. In the library, working on the manuscript of ancient mystical wisdom entitled *The Knowledge of the Knowers,* she could close him out, but at night, in her bedroom, he haunted her. Once she dreamt that he was standing over her bed, and called his name aloud. She woke, and in her dream-clogged state she seemed to feel his essence all around her.

If only she could have been sure she could trust him....

It didn't help that Sir John was constantly talking about his time in Bagestan and Parvan, reminding her of her own past, and the links she now had to the area. She wouldn't be able to run away forever. When whatever it was was over, if it ever was, she was going to have to deal with the family and her inheritance.

Several times she was on the point of asking Sir John if he knew the Bahrami family, or the al Makhtoums. Sometimes she had the feeling that he was waiting for something from her. But she was always held back by the thought that such questions from her would inevitably lead to questions from him, and to having to explain things to him.

For all she knew, Sir John might know the very people Najib said were looking for Sam.

She got into the habit of rising early on fine mornings and going out to wander for an hour before breakfast, hoping to find the standing stone. In the southwest quadrant of the property the woods were thick and very old, and while some paths ran right to the high stone wall that bounded the estate, others simply petered out in the middle of the woods.

She headed that way again, but this morning her mind was less on the mysterious compulsion of her forebears to stand stones upright in the forest than on a problem she had not considered before she laid such an elaborate false trail and disappeared—how she was going to find out when the danger was over and she and Sam could safely return to their lives.

She was following the course of a gurgling stream through the ancient forest as she pondered. The trees she slipped past were those which had been sacred to the Mother Goddess long ago—aspen, oak, ash, hawthorn, and elm, and the sun dappled through their branches onto the forest floor, making every spot sacred. She might almost be walking into the past, stepping back through the centuries to a time when the forest was new, her head so clouded with thought that she lost that firm grip on her reality and slipped through to another....

There was a place at which the stream broadened and, stirred in its journey by a sudden twisting of rocks and massive tree roots, rushed into a series of tiny rapids. The path ended at a large tree on its bank, and the wood behind was thick with brambles and holly.

Rosalind recognized it as the point where she had several times turned back, but she was wearing a short dress and the morning was very warm and, her mind elsewhere, she decided to press on. Sir John had said the way to the stone was not easy.

She bent and slipped off her shoes and, carrying them in one hand, clutched at the thick low branch the tree offered her and stepped down into the water.

It was deeper than she had thought, the hem of her skirt just brushing the surface. The water was ice-cold, but the bottom was pebbly and her footing felt secure. With the low branch as her support, she climbed carefully over one or two of the thick, gnarled black roots that twisted half across the stream, and then clutched the broad ancient trunk of the tree itself.

She passed under a branch, came around the tree,

and saw, thirty feet away through the trees, the rough circle of a clearing, bright with early sunshine. And on the edge of the clearing, in the shade of a great oak, was, unmistakably, the standing stone.

She could almost feel its power from here. Her mouth open, Rosalind stood entranced. After a moment she came to, moved along the length of another helpful branch of the tree above her, out of the tangle of roots, and into shallower water. One heave on a branch brought her up onto the bank, and she stood staring. She had entered a place where magic still was deep in every part of nature.

She stopped only briefly in a futile attempt to wring out the hem of her skirt, and then, barefoot, and making no noise, she stepped towards the clearing and the stone.

It was the largest single standing stone she had seen, well over six feet. Broad at the base, curving up almost to a point at the top, it gave the unmistakable impression of a woman kneeling, her rounded thighs and massive buttocks resting on her heels. There was even a hint of arms, with hands resting on the lap.

She saw without surprise as she approached that the lap was a human-size seat. Come to the Great Mother, was the invitation. With a smile of wonder Rosalind crept forward, stepped into the dappled sunshine in the clearing, and stood staring at stone that seemed to pulse with life.

She was thinking of nothing at all, only sensing the deep compulsion to go and give herself back to the Mother, to seat herself in that lap and connect to the wisdom that was there. She approached, feeling the rich fertility of nature all around her, and herself as part of the whole. The sensuality of moss on stone, of the leaves under her feet, of the green of the trees, the sun dappling the thick grass, was a primary, revealing without words how the world was being renewed by constantly recurring creation, the forever intertwining of male and female, the cycle of birth and death, sex and spirit.

In her state of altered awareness the movement near the stone seemed only part of it all, the life of the universe. When a shape detached itself from the Great Mother, when she saw a tall, dark man gazing at her from the shadows that danced over Her stone, he seemed a necessary part of the vision she was experiencing. Some part of her recognized the ancient truth that male and female called to each other in Her presence, and that Rosalind's own presence had of necessity summoned up the male.

But she was completely unprepared for the fact that the man was Najib al Makhtoum.

Seven

A dozen conflicting emotions attacked her at once. She wanted to run, she wanted to stay, she wanted to scream…she wanted to seduce him. Rosalind had a sudden vision of how the ancients had worshipped at this stone, soliciting the Great Mother for fertility of the fields and of the womb, and felt a wild compulsion to repeat that rite with Najib.

He still stood in Her shadow, wearing loose black trousers and a black polo neck shirt, and the skin of his firmly muscled arms and face was tanned. In the Celtic tradition, dark men brought good luck. A dark man should be the first across your threshold on New Year's Eve, to ensure luck throughout the year. And wasn't there some ancient tradition, Rosalind thought crazily, from before the time when people understood the full role of men in reproduction, that sex with a dark man would bring fertility to a barren woman as well as to the fields where they lay?

So the voices of the ancient gods of the place whispered in her, tempting her to the rite they loved best.

Rosalind turned and fled.

She ran barefoot through the thick grass, and the dark pursuer was caught off guard for a moment, so that she gained a lead. The gods settled to watch with satisfaction, for it was right that the maiden tested the man, and they loved the chase. Aspen and oak, holly and hawthorn trembled as she passed, and now and then a blossom blew into her path, or tumbled on her hair, for flowers were ever a part of the sacred rite....

Holly scratched the girl's strong bare legs, drawing stripes of blood on her flesh, and all trembled in anticipation of that other, virgin blood that would soon paint her thighs. But still they urged the brambles to catch the man and hold him, for the chase was delicious and they would prolong it if possible. It was so long since humans had thought to please them in this way....

The madness led her this way and that with perfect precision, and at last she obeyed the necessity and ran headlong back into the same clearing, where the grass was soft and suitable for a bower, where wildflowers danced in the wind, where the Goddess waited. And then, obedient to the gods' will, the grass tied itself against her foot, and the maiden was flung full length on the green bed, ready for the offering.

The dark man was close behind now, and needed no prompting from grass or root to fling himself down beside the girl as she tried to rise, his dark arm embracing her with the strength the Goddess loved. The girl rolled and struggled still, for the man must prove his power to the Goddess before she submitted.

They gave him what encouragement was fitting. The grass caught her skirt and tumbled it up around her hips, and wildflowers dressed her massy hair, and a blossom kissed her luscious, wanting mouth as they struggled in the grass.

"Don't be such a fool," Naj cried. "I am not here to hurt you!"

His voice cut through the crazy panic that had consumed her, and Rosalind lay still in his grasp, subsiding into the thick grassy carpet. She looked up into his face, panting hard.

"How—how did you—find me?" she asked.

His arm was stretched across her, his hand clasping her side just behind her breast. He lay above her, his gaze snared by hers, her panting breast beating against his hand, as if he had captured a wild animal.

"I had to find you," he said in his throat, and rivulets of feeling sprang up to trace over her skin and flesh. Her body twitched spasmodically.

"Najib," she protested, but under the protest her voice quivered with desire. For a moment they were still. The only movement came from a soft breath of wind like a sigh over the grass of the little clearing, and two pink blossoms that flung themselves against her cheek and lips. One rested tantalizingly at the sensitive corner of her mouth, but when she lifted a hand to brush it away, his hand prevented her.

Slowly, agonizingly slowly, he bent his lips to the blossom, and kissed it with a tenderness that sent a shaft of feeling, painful with intensity, shooting through her. Her breath sobbed and she closed her eyes, not to see, then opened them again because she had to.

Slowly, slowly, the dark man clenched his fist in her thick hair, then unfurled strong passionate fingers again to cup her head as his lips whispered from the petals of the flower to her cheek, so softly she did not know whether it was his lips or the blossom that brushed her, nor did his lips know whether it was her cheek or the flower they kissed with such tender passion. Again she closed her eyes.

His lips, or the petals, moved over her cheek, the bridge of her nose, between her eyebrows, over her trembling eyelid. Slowly her arms twined up the strong trellis of his own arms, and her hands pressed against his neck and into his thick hair.

His wandering, tender lips, with painful sweetness, traced their way back to the blossom of her mouth. He lifted his head then, and she opened her eyes, and they gazed into each other, half drunk. Then his mouth moved closer and slowly, slowly, their lips touched, tasted, and drank.

They lay entwined in a fast-flowing river of sensation. It coursed through them without mercy, and stirred into little rapids wherever their bodies met. Her fingers threaded his hair, pressing his mouth against hers with a hunger so deep it seemed to come from the earth itself. His hand pressed her side, stroked her breast, burnt its way down to her hip, and found her naked thigh, her bent knee. Her flesh was firm, her skin smooth, warm from the sun. His fingers slipped around under her knee and, his thumb stretched wide to clasp her, ran down the long line of her thigh, past the tickling grass to her hip.

Meanwhile his tongue toyed with the corners of her

mouth, his teeth nibbled the lips, and then, as if this stirred him too deeply, his other hand left her hair, moved to imprison her chin and throat, and his mouth possessed her lips again with rough hunger.

She heaved a breath when he lifted his lips, and opened her eyes with lazy pleasure. His thumb came to rest in the sensitive space where leg met body, and his fingers lazily curled around and trailed back up her inner thigh, making her yearn for more.

And then, with curious abruptness, the world returned. Who was he? She didn't even know him. She didn't know what he really wanted.

"My God, what are we doing?" she cried, as panic of a different kind stirred her.

Najib smiled, his teeth strong and white against his tanned skin.

"Don't you know?" he murmured, still absorbed in the mood that had captured them.

"Let go of me," the maiden panted. The watchers trembled with surprise. A wildflower flung itself against her cheek, to remind her of her duty.

"Rosalind," he whispered urgently.

"Let go."

The warm wind that had been twining her hair into the grass died, the leaves of the trees stilled, as if for a moment nature held her breath. Naj closed his eyes and heaved a deep sigh, then released her and rolled over on his back, his breathing fast.

Rosalind pushed herself up to a sitting position, wondering what the hell had got into her. The wind returned, stronger and with a chill in it. She pulled her wet skirt down over her bare thighs and shivered as the wild mix of fear and sexual arousal in her ebbed.

"How did you get here?" she demanded, turning

to look down at him. A cloud drew over the sun, and he dropped his arm and gazed up at her.

"How did you know where to find me?" she repeated.

The expression on his face made her gasp. He hadn't moved, but Rosalind was drawn to his hunger as if he dragged her with his arms. She jerked back, resisting the compulsion in her blood, and rolled to her knees.

"In this wood, because I followed you. In this place—" He lifted his arm, bent with his elbow resting in the grass, to gesture in the direction of the house. "I knew you were here because I brought you here."

She reeled as if he had struck her. "You—*what? You* brought me? How ridic—*how?*" She demanded again, and a cold dread began to weave through the unfamiliar pattern of emotions that wrapped her. "How did you bring me here?" she asked, her voice rasping.

Overhead the cloud that had obscured the sun was very quickly building into something threatening. Rosalind glanced up uncertainly and shivered again as the temperature in the little clearing seemed to plummet.

"Sir John is a very old friend of my family. Naturally he was concerned for your safety and that of your son. You are safe here only temporarily, however. It is not possible to secure this estate as tightly as is necessary. Other steps must be taken now."

His words were causing a dread in her like suffocation. "Do you mean he only hired me because... What steps?"

"Perhaps we should save the discussion." Najib

flung himself to his feet in one quick, graceful movement. "It is going to rain."

"Ow!" cried Rosalind, as the first drop struck her on the arm with unpleasant force, and then she saw tiny white balls bouncing on the grass. *"Hail!"* she cried in an incredulous voice. "It's *hailing!*"

"Let us get under cover," Naj muttered, helping her to her feet. She was shivering now, her wet dress gluing itself to her thighs uncomfortably as the hail flattened the grass. The wind whipped the hailstones against them with a certain malice, and they ran into the woods towards the narrow path she had fled along before and stopped under a tree.

"How weird that I came right back to the same clearing," she murmured, staring back into the clearing. "Where's the stone?" The Mother had disappeared. "It should be—"

"It is there," Naj said. "But it is not easy to see from this direction."

Rosalind stared in amazement. He was right. The stone was there, but from this angle, the colours blended in with the trunk of the huge oak behind it, and unless you knew what you were looking for, the Goddess seemed to be no more than a part of the gnarled tree.

"No wonder people don't find her," she murmured.

The angry hail battered the world, but amongst the trees they were spared the worst of it. Naj led her along a narrow path. She was only faintly surprised when the one they were on met the river path she had taken before.

"How did you know I would find the standing stone today?" she asked, with a return of paranoia, but he only shook his head.

"I did not know. But the path you took ends at the tree, and the choice is to turn back or go into the river. If you go into the river you find the stone. You have come this way several times, it was possible this time you would go on."

"Have you been following me every day?" she half shrieked.

He glanced at her without answering.

"Why?" she cried, and again he made no answer.

"Where are you staying?" she demanded next.

"In the bedroom next to yours, Rosalind!" he replied impatiently, turning to grasp her arms. "Have I not told you that you and Samir are in danger? Do you imagine that I would let you wander the world, vulnerable and knowing nothing of where the danger is thickest? Don't be a fool!"

She blinked under the storm of words. She didn't know how to answer, so she said nothing, and he dropped his hands and they went on in silence through the ancient wood.

"I want an explanation," she said at last.

He glanced down at her without breaking stride. He looked grim. "You will get one."

They came out of the wood and paused for a moment, looking at the sweep of lawn that led towards the house. It was a beautiful building, long and elegant, and she was more used to seeing this lawn from the other direction. There was no hail here. The dark cloud seemed to have departed, and the sun had risen above the trees now and was warm on the grass. The library windows, at the front of the wing that jutted out on the left, glittered.

"I've lost my shoes somewhere," Rosalind realized absently.

He only shook his head and led her across the grass towards a small door over to the right. It had once been a servants' entrance. Now it was the place where jackets and wellies were left, the paved stone floor having coped with mud for generations. In the tiny washroom off to the side, Rosalind quickly washed her feet in warm water, and wiped the blood from bramble scratches she didn't remember getting.

Naj was waiting when she came out again, still barefoot.

"Come," he said, and turned to lead her along the little hallway to a door at the end, where another hall ran at right angles. Here the floor was gleaming, polished oak, covered with a Parvan carpet runner. The jackets lining the walls gave way to art.

Najib seemed very familiar with the house. He led her in silence through the halls till she saw that they had come to the door into the library. He opened it, and closed it behind them, then led her across the familiar space, up to one of the portraits that Sir John had pointed out to her on her first day here.

"Do you recognize this man?" Naj asked her, breaking the silence at last.

"Yes, it's Hafzuddin al Jawadi," she said. "The old Sultan of Bagestan, who was overthrown by Ghasib in 1969."

Naj looked at her with an expression that frightened her. "I am glad you recognize him," he told her flatly, "because you have hated him for five years. This is the man who wrote you the letter."

Eight

"**B**reathe!" a deep voice insisted. "Rosie, breathe!"

She opened her eyes and recognized the brocade of one of the window seats under her thighs. Najib's hand was on the back of her neck, holding her head down between her knees.

Breath burst into her paralysed lungs. "I'm all right," she muttered, and then more firmly, "I'm all right."

His hand released her and she sat up, looking around at surroundings that seemed weirdly unfamiliar for a moment. Naj was leaning against the window embrasure, watching her with dark unreadable eyes.

"I've never done that before," she murmured, putting a hand to her forehead. "Phoo!" She blew her breath out, trying to relieve the sudden headache in her temples.

"You're just one surprise after another, aren't

you?'' She rubbed the back of her neck. ''Is it true? About him?'' She nodded towards the portrait.

''Of course it's true!'' he said impatiently. ''Why would I lie about such a thing?''

''I don't know,'' she said levelly. ''I don't know why any of this has happened. I feel as though I'm in a James Bond movie or something.'' She tried to ease her neck; it seemed to have seized up with shock. ''Why did you tell me like that? My God—Jamshid was Sultan Hafzuddin al Jawadi's grandson? Why didn't you—?''

''I'm sorry. My judgement had been disturbed,'' he said levelly.

She suddenly remembered that insane scene in the woods, and embarrassment stabbed her. Never again would she doubt the thesis that odd corners of the earth have strange powers....

''Who—'' She coughed and heaved a sigh. ''Who was Jamshid, then?''

''His birth name was Kamil. He was the only son of Crown Prince Nazim. An infant at the time of the coup. He was smuggled out of the country to Parvan when his father was murdered.''

''Dear God in Heaven!'' she whispered. ''The son of Prince Nazim? He—he would have been the...the next...''

''Without the coup, Prince Kamil would have been sultan one day,'' he agreed. ''There were many who hoped he might still be so.''

''The refugee groups,'' she said. Everyone knew that most Bagestanis in the West lived for the day the monarchy was restored and they could go home.

''The whole country,'' he corrected her.

No wonder he had said Jamshid had no right to marry her.

Silence fell again as he let her absorb it all. She sensed him move to the old-fashioned bell rope and pull it, and a moment later he issued a low-voiced instruction to one of Sir John's servants.

To the manner born. Of course. He too was a grandson of the sultan.

"Are you the sultan-in-waiting yourself now?" she asked as he returned.

"I? No."

"Why not?"

He hesitated. "Others have a better claim."

"Do you wish you could?" she asked curiously.

"I have no desire to sit on my grandfather's throne."

She didn't question that. It wasn't a fate she would choose in a million years. Rosalind plucked absently at the still-damp hem of her dress. "How could he marry me without telling me? Why didn't he—?"

"It is impossible to say. Perhaps when you got pregnant he felt his duty to you and the child was paramount."

"But why didn't he *tell* me? He never gave the slightest…" A thrill of horror went over her as she imagined how she would have felt if Jamshid had told her, after the fact, who she had married.

"Would you have married him if he had done so?" Najib asked.

She flicked him a startled look, then turned her eyes away. "I don't know. I…I loved him, but if there was any chance of him actually becoming sultan…" She shook her head. She was a private person and always had been. "I would have hated that so much."

He looked at her. He understood his cousin, but he could not explain to her how her femininity and beauty might drive a man to want to bind her to him, no matter what the future cost....

"Perhaps that is why he did not tell you."

She got to her feet and stood looking out at the green expanse of lawn.

"Sultan Hafzuddin had three wives," she remembered. "Is that right?"

"Yes."

"How do you all fit in?"

He said easily, "Rabia, his first wife, was a Quraishi, related to the Barakat royal family. She had two boys, Wafiq and Safa. Sonia was a Frenchwoman, daughter of the Comte de Vouvray. She had three girls, Muna, Zaynah and Yasmin. Maryam, his third wife, was a Durrani, related to the ruling family of Parvan. She was the mother of Nabila and of Nazim. You already know that Nazim was Hafzuddin's favourite and nominated to succeed him."

Standing with her back to him, she half turned her head "My mother is Yasmin," he said, in answer to the unspoken question. "My grandmother is Sonia, Hafzuddin's French wife."

Her chest seemed frozen. Rosalind took a long, deliberate breath. A deer stepped delicately out of the woods onto the lawn. In a voice that was suddenly expressionless, he went on.

"My grandfather had an adopted son, as well. His name was Ghasib. Perhaps you have heard the story. Grandfather saw him in the street one day when he was a child—an urchin, an orphan, who scrambled through rubbish heaps for his food. He was playing at war with some other street children—he impressed my

grandfather with a strong sense of his abilities. Hafzuddin adopted the boy, sent him to school and military college, trained him for power.''

Behind the resolutely level tone it was possible to
sense deep-rooted anger and pain.

''Nothing trained him in loyalty, however. In 1969,
Ghasib, the man who now calls himself Supreme President of Bagestan—'' Najib's voice was dry with con-
tempt ''—was my grandfather's commander in chief
of all the armed forces. You must have studied the
history.''

''Yes.'' She knew the history, but as something in a
book. Not as the story of her husband's family's life....

Ghasib was an orphan, but he had had a brother and
plenty of cousins. One by one he had brought them
into the military, given them positions of power. Under their leadership the entire military save the Royal
Guard was loyal to Ghasib. On the day of the coup
they surrounded the palace, the parliament, all the
main public buildings.

Crown Prince Nazim was killed in the first moments
of the assault on the palace. Princess Hana saw her
husband shot down, and pretended to be a servant. It
was said that she washed the shirts of her husband's
killers for a week before she was able to escape from
the occupied palace, taking her infant son in a bundle
of laundry. Loyal subjects helped to smuggle her and
her son to Parvan, her homeland.

Princess Hana was her own mother-in-law. Rosie
could hardly take it in.

''But there are things you cannot know, for they
figure in no history book,'' Najib said. ''Soon after the
coup, Safa was killed by an assassin. To protect his
remaining heirs, my grandfather ordered that the

whole family should take assumed names and go into hiding. Hana went to the mountains, where she took the name of a tribe which has always been loyally linked with the Durrani, and Kamil Durrani ibn Nazim al Jawadi Bagestani became Jamshid Bahrami when he was four years old.''

Rosalind watched the deer pick her delicate way across the lawn and stop again, large ears flicking this way and that, then lower her head to nibble a small plant. The sun was breathtakingly beautiful on the rich, brown pelt. So tender, so fragile. Her heart seemed to break with love for the delicate majesty of the animal.

''Not everyone could disappear so effectively. My Uncle Wafiq was killed in 1977, leaving two sons. The fact of his death was revealed by the family only in 1984, and the cause was said to be a heart attack. If it had been confirmed that the Jabir al Muntazir whom Ghasib had had killed was in reality Prince Wafiq al Jawadi, his sons would have been endangered. They are now the nearest to the throne.''

He stopped speaking, and silence fell on them, heavy and suffocating. Rosalind wandered back to the portrait, and they stood side by side looking at it. She glanced up into Najib's face, and at his nearness the memory of what had almost happened in the forest stole over her. He moved a little away, as if he felt the pull, too.

''This,'' Najib said, pointing to a ring on the sultan's hand, ''is the al Jawadi Rose. By tradition it was passed on from the sultan to his designated heir on the day he was appointed. Jamshid—Prince Kamil—was given this ring by my grandfather on his twenty-first birthday. It has disappeared.''

It was massive, too big for a ring. A fat circle running from knuckle to knuckle.

"And you thought Jamshid gave it to me?"

"Did he?"

"I've never seen it or anything like it. Didn't you say it was a diamond? It doesn't look like a diamond in the painting."

"It is a very rare pink diamond, cabochon cut," he said. "It's very old. Diamonds are not cut in cabochon today. Sixty-three carats."

She almost laughed. "Sixty-three! Well, you can be sure Jamshid never even showed me such a thing!"

Rosalind glanced from his face to that in the portrait. The portrait had been painted when the sultan was still relatively young, perhaps forty, and the face was impressive for its strength and intelligence. There was a certain family resemblance, most noticeable when a particular expression occurred in the eyes. And it was shared by Sam. She hadn't realized until now just how much Sam and Najib resembled each other.

Well, no surprises there.

"Can you understand my grandfather a little, now, Rosalind? He was a good and just ruler, but that did not save him from betrayal by the man who most owed him loyalty. One by one his three sons were murdered. And then there were the long, tortured years of hoping his grandsons would be allowed to grow to manhood.

"And then—Jamshid returned from England to announce that he would go to war at Prince Kavian's side. A wanton risking of his life, my grandfather said. His life was not his to risk. Prince Kamil al Jawadi owed his life to his own people.

"His death was the last blow. My grandfather was broken by it, as by nothing else that had occurred.

When he wrote you that letter, Rosalind, he was no longer himself.''

Silence fell. After a moment, she asked, ''And Jamshid—was he assassinated, too?'' she whispered.

''No. Jamshid was killed because he fought bravely.''

Rosalind licked her lips and turned to him. ''What now? Why is Samir's life suddenly in danger, if no one knew that Jamshid…''

''They did not know then, Rosalind. But we are almost certain that Ghasib now has the name Jamshid Bahrami as being one of the names taken by Hafzuddin's heirs. It is a stroke of good fortune that we discovered the will—and you—when we did.''

''Did you lead him to me?''

''No. But the first thing he will do is have investigators track Jamshid's life, to see if he left an heir. Unless we take steps to prevent it, he will unquestionably find you.''

Find her. Ghasib, the world's favourite demon. A man who, it was said, had thought nothing of killing his own brother when he suspected him of disloyalty. Rosalind took a deep, terrified breath and turned away.

The deer had disappeared. As if from a distance, she heard her voice say, ''And what will happen when he finds us?''

Without answering, Najib took her through a door that led from the library into the adjoining room, what Sir John called the small breakfast room. Breakfast had been laid out. The butler was setting a pot of coffee on a little table beside an expanse of window. On the sideboard were several dishes under silver lids.

They exchanged greetings as Rosalind sat. The butler tweaked a fork, bowed and withdrew.

Najib poured her coffee and set it in front of her. She needed it. She was in a state of shock. Shock upon shock. Rosalind stirred sugar into her cup, took a healthy slug, and felt a little revived. She set her cup carefully down and looked at the dark man sitting opposite. He seemed more of a stranger now. Grandson of a sultan.

"Tell me," Rosalind said, although the last thing she wanted to know was that the Supreme President of Bagestan was going to try to kill her son.

"Ghasib is not a sane man. If he comes to the conclusion that a grandson of Crown Prince Nazim exists he will feel very threatened. We must prevent this at all costs."

Rosalind's cup rattled in the saucer. Her hand was trembling like an old woman's. She *felt* like an old woman. Fear made you old.

"The important thing," Najib continued, "is that while he knows that Jamshid Bahrami was the assumed name of one of the heirs of Hafzuddin, Ghasib is not yet certain who Jamshid Bahrami really was. We may be able to confuse his investigations."

"How does he know the name?" she demanded.

Najib shrugged. "We can't be certain, but you have only to think about it. Ghasib's mismanagement of the water resources and agriculture in Bagestan last year produced another terrible crop failure. Hungry people may betray their own honour, Rosalind. Be grateful if you have never had cause to learn that fact."

He seemed a very different man now. He was not gentle anymore. Incisive intelligence was his dominant trait at the moment. She wondered suddenly what work he did.

"All right, if he finds out, what then?"

"He would have two choices. Ghasib has no son of his own, and since his brother's death has named no successor. If he is sane enough to see it, the intelligent option would be to take Samir under his 'protection,' to say that he himself is merely governing as regent, waiting for Sam to reach the age where he can rule. I am sure I don't have to explain the great advantage this would give him. You know how unpopular he is."

Naj paused to refill their cups. He picked up his and watched her over the rim until her eyes met his. "If he also has the al Jawadi Rose, the symbol that would prove Samir the designated heir of Prince Kamil, he is virtually unassailable."

"And is he smart enough to see it that way?"

"He might be made to see it. Armed with the information you now have, Rosalind, you could go to Ghasib. No doubt he would offer you the moon and sky to go to Bagestan and play the role of happy, trusting mother of the sultan-in-waiting. But you would have to deliver your son's safety into his keeping. It would be a great risk. Even if Ghasib himself intended Samir to be his heir, there are too many nephews and cousins already in contention. Samir's chances of ultimately becoming sultan would be very small."

He was looking at her questioningly, and she stared at him and frowned.

"Are you seriously asking me if I would go to a monster like Ghasib and offer him my son in return for—for—what? The chance to wear diamonds and drive around the desert in a Rolls? The chance to be mother of the Sultan of Bagestan one day? My God!" she exploded wrathfully.

"I am sorry. But how could I know how you would take the news?"

"Well, if you've been watching us as closely as you say you have, you might have noticed that I love my son!" she snapped.

"Rosalind, the world is full of people who imagine that they have a spoon long enough to allow them to sup with the devil in safety."

She subsided. It was true—he didn't know her, and how could he? She couldn't even tell him the single, central truth of Sam's existence.

There were appetizing smells coming from the serving board, and to gain time Rosalind got up and helped herself to egg and sausage and sautéed potatoes. Najib followed her lead, and for the next few minutes they ate without speaking.

What he had said sank in as she ate, and at last she looked at him. "I have to choose, don't I?" she said, as the chilling truth came home to her. "That's what all this has been about. There's no way to get away from it. I have to cast my lot either with you or with Ghasib."

He would not play games with her. "Yes."

She shook her head as anger at the stupid injustice of the whole situation crept over her. "Well, you've told me what Ghasib's best offer will be. You'd better tell me what yours is. I assume you've got one."

She glanced down at the fabulous diamond-and-ruby ring she was wearing, then lifted her hand to show it to him. "In fact, you might almost say I've already had the down payment!"

"Do you think we did not see this as a problem?" he said, his voice grating with irritation. "What were we to do? The will was found, you have inherited. We cannot keep your inheritance from you for the sake of not looking as though we wish to bribe you!''

She laughed angrily. ''What's your offer?''

But she was not only, or even primarily, angry with him. He was just handy, and Rosalind had too much natural justice to blame Najib for a situation that he had not created. The original fault was Jamshid's, for never having told her of this. And she was angry at fate, too, and at Lamis. Why hadn't Jamshid's cousin warned her?

''Our first priority is to get you to a safe house.''

She looked around. ''I thought you'd already done that.''

He shook his head firmly. ''No. It would be very much better if you would agree to come to Barakat. This option is a very poor second.''

''Why?''

He looked at her in surprise. ''Because in Barakat we have the resources of the state behind us. There you will be protected by the army if necessary.''

''The army? *What* army?''

''The Barakati armed forces. I am Cup Companion to Prince Rafi. Do you think the princes of the Barakat Emirates have no interest in the fate of a family to whom they are so intimately linked by marriage and blood?''

She was silent. He saw panic in her eyes. But there was no help for it. Now he had told her. She had to be convinced.

''Our focus at the moment is to prevent the discovery that Jamshid Bahrami was Prince Kamil.''

''How are you going to do that?''

''By a campaign of disinformation.''

She felt as though she was wandering deeper and

deeper into a maze until she had no hope of finding her way out.

"Disinformation?" she repeated hoarsely.

He paused. "There is one thing you must understand, Rosalind. If we do this, you may lose forever the opportunity to establish Samir's claim to the throne of Bagestan. He is young now, but as the only grandson of Crown Prince Nazim, in a dozen years he would be a very popular choice to spearhead a movement to replace Ghasib. If we now create an alternative history for him, it might be difficult to throw off later."

"I would be very happy to create an alternative history for him, if you can convince me someone would believe it. You don't seem inclined to believe his true history!"

"Rosalind," he said urgently, ignoring that, "will the day come when Samir regrets what we now do? Will he be angry that we have taken away his chance to challenge Ghasib for the throne of Bagestan?"

Rosalind's heart was sinking further with every word. God, what a fate! She hadn't thought of the real possibilities before. She tried to imagine how that would cripple Sam's life—to be sitting around wishing he were Sultan of Bagestan, conspiring, intriguing, flattered into waiting by refugee groups...

"Since I can't convince you that Sam actually has no right to the throne because he is not Jamshid's son," Rosalind said bitterly, "maybe you'll believe instead that I would do almost anything to prevent a life like that for him. What's your solution?"

"Our solution, Rosie," he said, his voice so quiet suddenly that she had to strain to hear, "is to pretend that Samir is my son."

Nine

Rosalind discovered she was no longer capable of reaction. There had just been too many shocks in the
past hour. Something in her finally accepted that the
world was not in any way as she had imagined it. If
the wall of the room parted and Sultan Hafzuddin
stepped through to rain curses on her head, she
thought, she would feel no surprise.

She found that this made her stronger. Freed from
her preconceptions, she could now react to events as
they occurred, as they were, rather than first measuring
them against what life should be. Maybe this was what
they meant by the dance to the music of time.

"And how will we do that?"

"By proceeding as if I were the man who met and
married you five years ago."

Her breath escaped in a rush. "Would that work?
Don't too many people know the truth?"

able thing Rosalind had in such abundance, a thirst that seemed to have been lying by his heart unrecognized all his life. He had been reasonably satisfied. Now he had discovered the elixir of life, and his own long-standing thirst for it, and in the same moment knew that he could not taste it.

It was an annoyance, but that was all it was. He wasn't going to let it get to him. Hunger and thirst, whether physical or spiritual, was something you could ride out. That was a lesson you learned on the battlefield.

Rosalind saw the wariness in his eyes, and sighed. Whatever his reasons for resisting the attraction, she was pretty sure she was looking at heartache if she tried to break through that resistance. His eyes were not the eyes of a man who has permanence on his mind. They weren't even the eyes of a man who is comfortable with a sexual attraction.

She tasted the erotically delicious food cooked by the well-meaning staff and wished that everything they were pretending were true. That Najib had come back to her after five lost years, loving her, the father of her son, and that they would go back to the bedroom and be true lovers on such a magical night....

"Oh, the stars are beautiful!" The words came out of her without her volition.

His jaw tightened. "Yes," he said. Then, as if on the heels of a thought, he asked, "Did Kamil—did Jamshid buy your apartment for you?"

He watched dispassionately as her eyelids dropped to hide her eyes from him and self-consciousness stained her cheeks.

Rosalind swallowed. "No."

"You inherited the money, perhaps?" Their search

showed that the place had been bought in Rosalind's name, no mortgage, four and a half years ago.

Rosalind set her fork down. She had never thought of being asked this question, and she had no answer ready to explain how an ordinary woman had been able to afford so wildly expensive an apartment....

"No," she said, because next he would ask from whom. She didn't think of the easiest course, to tell him it was none of his business, until too late. "It's not really mine."

What did this mean? The most likely explanation was that it had been put in her name, but she had signed it away in a document that could be held over her head, keeping her obedient. He could imagine Ghasib involved in a thing like that. If she betrayed him, she would find herself instantly homeless.

That argued that Ghasib had been consulted before she agreed to come here. That would mean Ghasib was hoping she would learn something of substance from him, Najib...and that she was willing to betray him. He looked at her, and his heart twisted with grief. His jaw tensed against the desire to rail at her.

The lamplight made her too beautiful. He pushed his chair back from the table. "Shall we walk?" he said.

Rosalind had only been toying with the remains of the delicious dessert, and she obediently dropped her spoon and got to her feet before the servant could appear from the darkness to hold her chair.

Naj led her through the house out into the walled garden. He sensed the approving smiles of the staff following them, and slipped his arm around her back as he ushered her out, feeling as he did so how much he wanted to be her protector. But if she was collaborating with Ghasib, no one could protect her.

Well, they would walk under the stars and the staff could imagine what they liked about what was passing. He dropped his arm as soon as darkness enveloped them. Here there were other eyes, but there was nothing to prove to them.

A cloud of intoxicating perfume rushed against her when they stepped into the garden. Rosalind caught her breath on surprised pleasure. ''Roses!'' she exclaimed. ''How on earth can you have so many plants?''

''There is a spring here. It is the reason the house was built on this spot,'' he answered mechanically. He did not smell the roses, but her hair. It had released its own scent to his nostrils as she swung her head. A clean smell, lemon rather than musk, but no less disturbingly sensual.

The darkness was lightening imperceptibly as they threaded their way along the paths, the silence between them alive with the unspoken. The glow behind the domed roof meant the moon was moving into view.

He thought of the morning when he had gone to her apartment. He had been swept by the desire to lift her in his arms without a word and carry her to her bed…he wished he had done it. He wished he had become her lover before he had been forced to suspect her of so much treachery.

He said, with a harshness that startled her, ''Does a woman feel guilty, taking a lover when her husband is at war?'' He said it to stop the trend of his own thoughts, but she heard it as an attack.

Her eyes glistened with indignation as they focussed

on him, reflecting moonlight. "You're very sure I know the answer to that."

"I am not sure!" he said, his voice like sandpaper. "I am sure of nothing with you, nothing! Only one thing I know—" he lifted a hand to punctuate every word with a stroke of his forefinger "—that you have not told me all the truth. No!" He cut her off when she would have interrupted him. "Do not deny it! You cannot deny it!"

She was silent, the angry denial caught in her throat.

"Tell me," he commanded softly, as temptation crept towards him again, like an animal scenting the fatally wounded in the desert. "Tell me the truth and I will love you, Rosalind. I will make such love to you—"

Her hand flew to her throat. "What?" she whispered.

He stroked light fingers down her bare arm. He *was* wounded, she had pierced his heart in the first moment she looked at him, suspicious and mistrustful though her eyes had been.

"You are a woman who enjoys sex, Rosalind. Do you think a man does not know such a thing?"

She closed her eyes and breathed to silence her noisy heart.

"I, too, Rosalind. And I look at you and know that I can give you lovemaking to remember. Days and nights, we would be drunk on our own pleasure. You will not regret it. Your body will sing for me...."

Sensation rippled through her like a shock wave. She swayed where she stood. "What are you saying?" she murmured, hardly hearing more than the word *lovemaking* in that deep, intimate, caressing voice.

"How my mouth craves to kiss you, Rosalind, my

hands burn with wanting to touch you. Do not you feel it? I know you do. I see it in your eyes. You want my touch. Tell me that it is so. Say it!''

''Najib,'' she whispered. Winds seemed to buffet her from every direction. Her body was streaming with feeling, with yearning, with deep need of his touch.

He had met the woman he had dreamed of, and she was a cheat. How could it be so? Why did she not give him an explanation that would release his desire from the restraint he had to place on it? How could such passionate need as he felt for her co-exist with the deep suspicion that she was a danger—to him, to the family, to the thing that ruled all their lives?

His hands gripped her shoulders, and with the sudden convulsion of a starving man, he bent to kiss her throat. Her head fell back on a moan.

He could make her confess. Lovemaking would be the undoing of a woman like her, he knew it. She moaned with the merest touch of his mouth. He could melt her utterly, she would be all his, and then she would tell him whatever he asked...so his demon whispered....

''Rosalind,'' he murmured. His strong hand tipped her head and his lips moved up under her ear, to a spot that suddenly proved to be connected to every nerve in her body. His hand ran down her side to her hip, to her thigh, with a ruthless pressure that spoke deep, passionate hunger.

She melted and gasped for air, and his mouth was suddenly clamped to hers, devouring her. She moaned and swayed against him.

Dimly, as his arms wrapped around her and dragged her ruthlessly against him, he realized that sex was a two-edged sword. He should not have tried to use against her a weapon that could so easily be turned against himself.

What if it is not her, but you yourself who confess all? the voice of reason cried urgently in him. *When she has defeated you with the pleasures of the body...can you be certain it is not you who will tell her whatever she asks?*

But the thought was drowned under the tidal wave of need.

Twelve

Moonlight streamed into the bedroom through the lattice, imprinting moving arabesques of light and shadow on the coverlet, the walls, the floor.

She moved ahead of him slowly, towards the bed, into the pale beams. Her hair swung, making its own moonshadow on the wall, and he felt even the movement of shadow to be a touch that was painful.

She was ghostly in the darkness, in the slender, pale dress, the darker skin, and he wanted her to be real. He lifted his arms and stripped off his shirt, tossing it into the shadows.

There was a sudden odour of his male sweat, and she gasped in erotic surprise and turned to take him in as he came nearer. His chest curved with muscle, and his dark skin was darker with the black hair that curled over chest and arms.

He had stepped out of his thonged sandals and approached her now in silence, his foot like a lion's paw, folding softly down onto the marble floor.

Her arms went around his waist and she pressed her face against his naked shoulder and smelled him again, skin, sweat, sun and soap all contributing to the heady aroma that was him.

He was everything she needed. So strong, so male, so real. Everything that had been missing from her life for too long.

His hands slid the zipper down her back and moved inside to caress her bare skin with a touch that electrified her. He buried his face in her hair, kissed her ear and, when her head fell helplessly to one side and then back, her neck and throat. One hand moved up to push the neckline of her dress out of the path of his seeking lips.

She felt his touch like a tracery of fire sending out rivers of flame over all her skin, through every muscle and cell. She kissed his chest, felt the curling hair brush her lips, too, with fire. She ran her hands over his back, feeling the firm musculature, the strongly knit spine.

He drew a little away, and his hand came up to tilt her chin back, raise her mouth for his kiss. For a moment they stopped, staring into the blackness of each other's eyes, and then his lips came down on hers. Electric heat spiralled out from the contact, and her body trembled in his hold.

His hold was firm and determined on her head, holding her just where he wanted her while his mouth took hungry possession of hers, so hungry she melted against his chest with a cry. Then, his lips firmly locking hers, his hands slipped down to encircle her, and

his arms wrapped her tight against him, secure, en-
closed, held.

He was in no hurry. Hungry he might be, but that
only made him the more determined to enjoy every
sweet, delicious morsel to the full. Inside the opening
of her dress again, his hands caressed her back, her
sides, the sensitive space under her arms, the swelling
of her breasts at the sides, his fingers stroking her
nerve endings into wilder and wilder disarray.

They stroked all down the length of her spine, and
then up again, and the touch seemed to release a fire
inside her that licked all up her spine with the most
delicious heat she had ever experienced.

His mouth nibbled and chewed and pressed and
toyed with hers, and his hands stroked her, till her skin
twitched convulsively all over and her body ached
with hunger. Then he abandoned her swollen lips and
trailed his mouth down the line of her neck again, to
the neckline of her dress, and now his hands pulled
the fabric away and down her arm, leaving her shoulder vulnerable to the trailing fire of kisses.

His tight hold on her relaxed, and his naked chest
moved away as he drew her dress down both arms.
For a moment she was imprisoned by the fabric of her
dress, her arms caught at her sides, and he held her
there and gazed at her with a look in his eyes that
melted her again and again in waves of electric heat.

His eyelids drooped as her naked breasts were
kissed with moonlight, and then he held her back over
his arm and bent to press his own kiss against that
moon-whitened skin.

Her dress tumbled down over her hips and to the
floor, and his other arm slipped under her knees, and

he picked her up out of the circle of white cloth and carried her to the bed.

She awoke to birdsong, her body lazy and luxurious, as if she had honey instead of blood in her veins. A thin sheet was all that covered her, and its touch on her supersensitive skin as she turned was erotic, as his hands had been, in the night.

She smiled, languidly stretching, and opened her eyes. Sunshine was playing through the lattice across the bed, the pattern moving as a little wind played with the branches outside. The scent of the desert came to her, bringing all its harsh beauty to her mind.

She was alone. She rolled over and buried her face in the pillow where he had slept, breathing in the smell of him as remembered pleasure shot through her body, melting her womb with yearning.

She showered and pulled on briefs and a cotton dress and sandals. In heat like this shorts were constricting. A long, loose dress allowed the air to circulate, and the dryness of the air meant sweat evaporated almost before it had a chance to form.

Out in the shadowed courtyard the morning was still relatively cool, and the air had a freshness and a purity that was delightful.

Najib and Samir were sitting at a table on the western side of the courtyard, where the sun's rays reached in under the cloister. Sam was babbling away and Najib was listening and nodding. Both were wearing the white Arab garment called djellaba, a simple full-length robe with long loose sleeves. Rosalind paused to watch them for a moment, her body rushing with the memory of the night.

They didn't notice her until she was gripped by a

sudden paroxysm of coughing, and then both turned
her way. Sam laughed and called out to her, but although Najib smiled, his eyes were grave.

Rosalind bent to give Sam a hug and kiss. She
wanted to do the same with Najib, but his look made
her a little nervous of him, and she only smiled her
good-morning. One of the staff pulled out her chair
and poured her a cup of coffee, then rolled up a trolley
for her choice of breakfast.

"I am wearing a dress, Mommy," Sam informed
her gravely. "Daddy is wearing one, too. Men wear
dresses in the desert."

"It looks very handsome," she said. There was
something majestic about a man wearing such a robe,
and Najib was certainly no exception. "But where did
you get it?"

"Tahira put it on me."

She glanced a question at Najib. "It is the most
comfortable wear for this heat," he said, and she assumed that meant that he had ordered it done.

They ate their breakfast, with Sam doing most of
the talking. He clearly liked the whole situation, from
the heat to the clear skies to the fact of sitting down
to meals with two parents. Rosalind watched with a
little pang how intimately he smiled into Najib's eyes,
and prayed that Najib would prove to be right—that
it would be better for them to bond, even if Najib were
later to disappear from Sam's life.

But the truth was she was hoping that he would not
disappear....

She mentioned the beach, and Najib said that it was
best to swim in the morning, because the sun would
be too intense later. So they spent a lazy time over the
breakfast table and then Rosalind slipped on a swim-

suit under her dress and they strolled down to the little cove.

It was very, very different from any beach Sam had ever been at before. She stripped off his djellaba and let him run into the water naked, and he cried, "Mommy, it's *warm!* The water is warm!" and flung himself into it with total abandon.

"I always thought he was a little nervous of the water," Rosalind told Najib. "I never realized before that it was a question of temperature!"

The little cove was mostly sheltered from ocean currents by the fingers of rock which were progressively longer on neighbouring coves. There were a couple of yards of shallows before the beach sloped steeply into deeper water. The surface was calm, the water lapping gently at the shore. For swimming it was almost ideal.

About twenty yards away from where they were, on one side of the cove, was a little stony outcrop, and after a while Najib took Sam on his back and set off to swim to it, with Rosalind beside them. Sam was laughing with delight, his little hands wrapped around Najib's neck, his head trustingly pressed against Najib's, gasping and blinking when water splashed him, but completely fearless.

Rosalind, doing a lazy crawl beside them, wondered what she would do with her inheritance. It was clear that Sam loved the climate, but how would he feel, how would they both feel, about coming here when Najib was not with them? There was no doubt that for Sam a big part of the perfection of the moment was Najib's presence.

For her, too.

"If I don't want to keep this place, what will happen?" she asked Najib later, when he was showing her over the house and grounds. They were in a small study off the other courtyard, where she had been surprised to discover a computer with an Internet linkup, and several phones. It meant she could work here and send in her translations by e-mail. If she wanted to.

He had just explained the presence of all this equipment by saying that the house had been a family holiday place for years. Sophisticated communications were necessary for many members of the family.

"You do not want the house?" he murmured, looking at her from under lowered brows.

His voice was expressionless. She couldn't tell what his attitude was. "Well, something in France would probably be more practical as a holiday home," she said. "It's so expensive to fly out here, and—"

"You and Sam of course travel free on Royal Barakat Air," he interrupted impatiently.

Rosalind blinked. "We do? Free? Why?"

"We are about to be married, Rosalind. As far as the world is concerned, we are married already. The families of the Cup Companions travel free on Royal Barakat Air."

"Oh," she said. And then, "But it's not even a real marriage."

She wasn't sure why she said it. Maybe to get a reaction from him. She certainly got one. Naj said, with obvious irritation, "How much more real does it have to get, Rosalind? We were husband and wife last night, were we not?"

The embers of awareness that were always there between them exploded into flame with a heat that seemed to suck all the air out of her lungs. He grasped her arm. "Do you—" he began, but whatever he had been going to say was lost as Rosalind, responding to that touch with a hunger that melted him, slipped into his embrace and tilted her face up for his kiss.

He had meant to resist. He had meant to explain how foolish it would be for them to continue what he had been helpless to prevent beginning. But her lips, already swollen with his last night's kisses, now parted in willing expectation, and it was too much for him. His mouth closed the gap of its own accord, and roughly drew the sweetness from hers.

He gave himself up to the madness that consumed him. He had awakened this morning with her warm, naked body stretched out beside him in the deep abandon of a woman who has been thoroughly pleasured in the night, and an almost overwhelming hunger to awaken her with more lovemaking had swept over him.

He had forced himself up and away. What good could come of this? One way or another, she was a betrayer. She had probably already betrayed him, the whole family, and she might prove their downfall in the end. But the physical need for her was affecting his judgement.

Kingdoms had been lost before this for the sake of a woman's love. And if the women had been like Rosalind, Najib reflected, with an appreciation he had never before felt for the dilemma of such fools, he could understand it.

Down on the beach they had both dressed and then slipped off their wet suits. He was naked under the djellaba, and he knew she was naked under the dress. It was too easy, it was impossible not to give in to what was offered. His hands caressed her with rough hunger, but she was already moaning with need. Her hands pulled at him, her body strained against his.

With a muttered oath, he turned her away, dragging up her loose dress, and she understood his design and bent over the back of the chair. The sight of her naked back was more potent than he could have dreamed in a thousand weeks of bliss, and he dragged his own robe out of his way and thrust into the waiting heat.

She cried out with wild excitement, a sound that tortured him almost into instant loss of control, and he clenched his jaw, his hands tight on her hips, for a motionless moment while he struggled against it.

One hand moved under her body, to find the cluster of nerves that had already proved so responsive to his touch, with one unerring finger.

Rosalind exploded into release, her throat opening to cry out her surprise, as the delicious heat spiralled out from under his hand and his driving body and then instantly began to build again.

It was a heat as searing as the desert sun, a blasting, merciless power. The world went black, and she floated there, battered by high, drowning waves of pleasure measured by each stroke of his body in her. She gasped for air after each one, and the thirst for release was cruel, she was lost at sea under hot sun, crying, hungry, battered, desperate—until he broke through with a high cry, and then it flowed through her like sweet water, a cooling bliss like nothing she had experienced before.

Thirteen

After that he gave in to it. It was impossible to do anything else. Between the tempting food, the primitive heat, the greenery, the cooling fountains, the sea, the child's steadily deepening trust of him, and Rosalind's languid, hungry smiles and languid, delicious body, he was a lost man and knew it.

Every morning and evening they swam in the cove. He taught Samir not to fear salt in his eyes or on his lips, or water in his nose, and watched his transformation into dolphin with deep pleasure. Or they put on masks and snorkels and, Najib and Rosalind carrying Sam between them on a sling, swam over coral beds to watch the fish feeding. Sam and Rosalind both were left amazed and wondering by the colour and variety and beauty of the underwater world.

There were goldfish in one of the reflecting pools, too, and Sam could spend hours lying on his tummy, watching and playing with them while his mother, sitting nearby, read some of the books from the shelves in the study.

Newspapers came in by helicopter a couple of times a week, and usually there was a bag for Najib, too. But Rosalind didn't bother much with the papers. She was taking a holiday from the real world. She did not want to know about politics or war or even whether she and Najib were a subject for the gossip writers.

Although she found the scenery compelling, Najib advised her against taking walks inland. The heat was too strong, and it would be very easy to lose her direction in such unfamiliar terrain. In the evenings, when Sam was in bed, he took her along the line of the shore, which in one direction could be traversed for almost a mile before one of the fingers of rock made it impassable. Along one side of the finger they could walk on the beach to the end of the tip jutting out into the sea, but around the other side the face was a sheer cliff down into the water.

High at the very fingertip of this mound was a cave. Inside, in the soft rock, someone had carved niches to create sleeping platforms. There was no way of knowing how long ago the humans who had done this had lived—thousands or merely hundreds of years ago. Yet there was a feeling in the place, as if of connection over a huge distance in time, to someone not so very unlike herself.

The cave had probably been chosen because it mostly faced east, getting the rays of the rising sun and avoiding the heat of the afternoon. But just outside there was a flat platform, probably once used for fire, where they could sit and watch the sunset, and feel their kinship with those other humans who had probably worshipped the sun as a powerful, dangerous father.

Once they made love there, high over the pounding waves, as the light turned from golden to orange to red, and then the night had enveloped them.

Rosalind had never been so happy, not since long-ago days of childhood, when her parents had taken her for carefree holidays on the Mediterranean and it had seemed to her that she would never have anything to trouble her.

Logic warned her this, too, was destined not to last. But what was the point of worrying about the future in such a magical present? Najib never said he loved her, but it was there in his eyes as he touched her, in his body when the pleasure was too much for them both. It was in his deep caring for Sam, that masculine mix of strength and tenderness that entranced the boy as well as his mother.

And if he sometimes seemed tortured when he turned to her, if it seemed that he wished he could resist the powerful chemistry they shared, but could not—well, what was that but a promise that, in the end, love would triumph?

"Look, Mommy!"

There was a narrow strip of beach in the neighbouring cove that, protected by a rock overhang, was in shadow as soon as the sun passed midheaven. Rosalind sometimes took Sam there with his bucket and spade during the afternoon. There was a large bowl-shaped rock shelf just underwater, and another shelf above, and in the heat of the afternoon it was pleasant in the shade, lying on the sand or sitting on the rock shelf with her feet in the water, while Sam played.

When she got hot she would slip down into the bowl and let the cooling sea wash her.

Usually she took a book, not from the library, but one of the paperbacks she had asked the staff to bring her from town on a supply run in the helicopter.

At the moment she was reading a thriller. She wasn't enjoying it very much; it was violent and unpleasant, but the writer wrote compellingly and she couldn't seem to stop reading it. She put it down as Sam called, and looked to see his latest sand creation.

"A boat!" he called. It didn't look much like a boat, unless it was a steamship that was sinking, with only two pail-shaped funnels still showing above the waves. Sam came up to where she was sitting on the beach and pointed out over the water, and Rosalind turned.

It was a boat, all right, a motor launch coming into view well outside the cove. Two men stood at the stern fishing, and waved as they saw her. Rosalind and Sam waved back. And just as she realized that the men were pointing something at them that glinted in the sun, the sound of a gunshot cracked the air, echoing loud off the cliffs around them.

She screamed. Screamed and grabbed Sam in the same breath, throwing him flat on the sand and piling on top of him, to protect him with her own body.

She craned to see behind her. The men had lowered their weapons and were looking away from them, over the water to the west. Sam was just starting to cry from surprise and shock.

"Sam, we have to get up and run," she said. "We have to run away from the bad men in the boat," she said urgently. "You hang on tight, Mommy will carry you. All right? *Go!*" she cried, and surged onto her

feet, her back still to the boat to shield him, grabbed
him under the arms, dragged him up, felt him cling to
her like a monkey, and started running.

But it was far, far too late for that. With hideous,
terrified astonishment, Rosalind saw that two other
men were coming at them from higher up the beach,
and there was no mistaking the lethal weapons they
were carrying as they ran down towards her.

When they saw her, one veered in her direction, but
he didn't raise his rifle, and, not wasting any breath
on screaming, Rosalind clutched Sam tight and just
kept on running. The gunman was shouting in Parvani,
''Get down!''

Sam was too shocked now to make a noise. Rosalind ran up the beach into the blinding sunshine, trying
to avoid the cutting rocks, towards the top of the finger. It was one way back to the house, over the finger
and down, but she knew she would be dangerously
silhouetted at the top.

As she crested the rise, she crouched over and, still
running, bent as low as she could to the ground.

On the other side of the finger, Najib was running
towards them at full tilt. ''Get down, Rosalind, get
flat!'' he shouted, and she obediently dropped down,
pressing Sam down and spreading herself over him
again. She was panting, her heart beating so hard it
seemed ready to explode. Sam was crying, the choked,
fitful wail of sheer terror.

''It's...*uh uh*...all...*uh*...right, dar...*uh*...ling,''
she panted when she could. ''Najib...is...''

And he was there, crouching over them in his white
djellaba, and she saw without surprise that he had an
automatic in his hand. He put his hand on her head,

signalling her to keep low. Then he found Sam's shoulder and grasped it.

"Sam, it's all right," he said. "I've got you safe."

"There were two men right on the beach," she warned him. "They have Uzis, I think."

He remained crouched there, looking into the distance behind her, and on all fours, spread low with Sam under her, Rosalind slowly slithered around so that she could see. She gasped.

"Who are they?" she cried.

There were now two boats in the water, much closer to shore than before. Both were motor launches, but there the resemblance ended. One was dark green and bristling with aerials and antennae, carrying several armed men. Three of them were levelling automatic rifles at the occupants of the white boat. In the white boat stood the two men she had first seen, their arms up over their heads, hands empty.

The green boat was slowly coming up alongside the white one, and as the gap closed, two of the armed men boarded. As she watched they handcuffed the occupants of the white boat, and then forced them, none too gently, into the second boat.

A man on the beach was talking into his radio; the other was now standing only yards away from Naj and Rosalind and Sam, legs apart, his gun in the ready position, his eyes combing the landscape.

Sam struggled, and she drew him up into her arms, and they sat silently watching.

One of the men who had boarded the white boat started the engine, and it scudded out into a turn to follow as the green one, its prisoners below, gunned its motor and set off. A moment later both boats disappeared from sight behind the angle of rock, then reappeared beyond the next cove, heading up the coast towards Daryashar.

Silence fell. The two men left on the beach approached them, still watchful.

"Let's get you into the house," Najib said, and bent to pick up Sam.

Her body was running with chills. She had never been so frightened in all her life, and she was bursting with questions.

So was Sam. "Were they bad men, Daddy?" he asked.

Whatever he was actually feeling, Najib was completely calm outwardly. He reached out his free arm and wrapped Rosalind in against his side as they walked.

"Well, we don't know, Sam. We'll ask them."

"Were the other men bad men, too?"

"No, the other men are soldiers. They came to protect you."

Sam babbled as the shock wore off and excitement started to take over. Najib held him firmly and spoke calmly all the way back to the house, and Rosalind felt how soothing his voice and presence were. He was calming her, too.

Outside the gate, their escort sketched a salute and turned away into the rocky landscape.

As the shock wore off, her feet suddenly started to sting. They were crossing the central courtyard when the housekeeper, Rima, came out behind and cried in horrified Arabic, pointing at the floor, "Who was wounded?"

Rosalind looked down and discovered that she had left a trail of blood over the tiles. Her feet had been cut on the rocks.

"Mommy's feet are bleeding!" Sam cried, with every evidence of satisfaction, and Najib and Rosalind both laughed. Rima rushed over, exclaiming, and nothing Rosalind could say would convince her that it was not important and she would wash the blood off in the shower.

No, Rima insisted, appealing to Najib's authority, Rosalind must allow her feet to be dressed, they must be properly tended against infection.

Eventually it was all over, her cut feet neatly cleaned and bandaged. She heard the helicopter come and go. But it wasn't till Sam had eaten his dinner, relived the excitement over and over, and at last gone to sleep that Rosalind had time to talk to Najib, and then he wasn't around. She went looking, and found him in the study, alternately answering the phones and talking on the radio.

She sat down and waited for him to be free.

"Have they been questioned?" she asked, when he hung up the phone again and turned to her.

"Yes. They say they are journalists, paparazzi. They have papers and the cameras to prove it. They wanted no more than to steal a few pictures in advance of the wedding."

Rosalind shook her head. "They fired a gun at us."

Najib frowned, his hand going instinctively to the phone. "How many shots did you hear?"

"One."

He relaxed. "The military boat fired across their bows."

"Oh," she said, and heaved a long, exhausted sigh. "Oh, thank God! Do you think they really are paparazzi?"

"My men say that they were badly frightened and

put up no resistance to being boarded. The film has been developed, a dozen or so pictures of you and Sam on the beach. The boat has been taken apart and there is nothing on it, no surveillance equipment, no weapons of any description. They rented it for the day from a local man in Daryashar who is now screaming for its return. He has no known connections to any political group.''

''Your men?'' she repeated.

Najib hesitated. ''The men detailed to guard you are secret service agents attached to the Palace Guard. They come under my purview.''

''I didn't know we were being guarded here.''

He looked at her. ''But I told you that was precisely why we wished you to come to East Barakat.''

She shrugged. ''I thought this place was far enough out of the way, and no one knew we were here....''

He shook his head, his jaw tight. ''Where did you get your professional training?'' he said, cutting across her.

She was completely thrown by the change of subject. ''My professional—do you mean, where did I take my language degree?''

''My men say you reacted with the instincts of a trained agent, Rosalind,'' he said impatiently, as if she were being wilfully naive. ''Where did you learn these skills?''

''A trained agent?'' she repeated incredulously. ''What do you mean?''

He looked at her. ''You protected Sam like a trained bodyguard, Rosalind,'' he explained.

''And that's enough to make you suspicious?'' she demanded hotly. ''Your men are too far removed from ordinary life! Try 'determined mother'! What do you imagine any mother would do if someone started shooting at her child?'' She was getting angrier as she spoke. She couldn't *believe* this! In spite of everything he was still in doubt about her motives! Their intimacy counted for exactly nothing.

He sat unmoved. His doubting silence infuriated her. Rosalind flung herself to her feet, staring across the desk at him.

''You imagine that because I instinctively protect my child I've been in one of Ghasib's terrorist training camps, is that it? Get a life!''

She whirled and stormed out.

Najib watched her go. He sat there for a long moment, ignoring the phone that had started to ring. He pulled open a drawer and drew out a photograph, from one of the photographers' films that had been developed.

In it, Rosalind was standing on the beach, looking towards the camera, her arm up in signal.

She had been expecting someone. Who?

The episode unsettled them, introducing the snake into their paradise. She couldn't escape from the knowledge that he had doubted her.

In one way she could hardly blame him. On the surface her story didn't fit reality. Yet in her heart Rosalind was disappointed. He didn't believe her, and that meant he didn't trust her.

He made such passionate love to her at night that until now she had hoped, or believed, that it was more than physical attraction. But if a remark from a secret service agent could pitch him into such doubt, what did it say about his feelings for her?

As for her own feelings for Najib, Rosalind was no

longer in any doubt. She was falling deeply in love, heart, mind, body and spirit. She was learning to trust him at the deepest levels of her being.

Sexually he was so giving, she could trust him so deeply. She could not have given herself up to the pleasure he gave her without trusting him. She found it bewildering to learn that he could make love to her at night, yet still harbour suspicions about her in the day....

He joined her for dinner as usual. It was her favourite time of day—when the heat of day was over, the night soft and scented all around them, she and Najib talking together.

But tonight there was a constraint between them. They did not talk so easily about little things. At night they often discussed incidents from Sam's day, the things he had said or done, and he laughed with her so warmly that she imagined he was becoming attached to Sam, too.

But tonight that was overshadowed by what had happened on the beach. Any mention of Sam brought up images too harrowing to contemplate.

When Najib's gaze rested on her tonight, there was a frown in his eyes, as if he wanted to pierce her soul and learn what was there. But she had already given him access to her soul. He knew what was there. How was it he did not recognize this? Apart from one secret that was not her own, there was nothing she would not share with him.

The discovery that he did not understand this was depressing. It said that she had been building castles in air. That her dreams had no foundation.

It tormented her, but he was tormented, too, tonight. Usually after dinner they walked for a while in the garden, but tonight there was a mutual silent understanding that they would not do so.

Rosalind went to the bedroom alone, feeling restless and unsettled. Today's events had brought home to her the truth of what she was doing and why. Up till now it had seemed more of a game. From the moment Najib al Makhtoum had first knocked on her door, she seemed to have been divorced from her real life.

But all those armed men had been real. Too real. They brought home to her what, she saw now, she had never really accepted in her heart before—that Najib and others really believed Sam's life might be in acute and immediate danger. They had obviously been under surveillance the whole time. Every time she and Sam had been outside the house, they had been watched.

He had said the danger would be over in a few weeks, and she had allowed that to lull her into thinking the danger might not be so real.

Now it suddenly seemed she had to reassess everything. But she didn't know what new interpretation to put on the facts.

It grew late and later, and still he did not come. She began to think he meant to sleep in another room. Rosalind tried to read, but the thriller she was in the middle of was filled with such dark motives and actions that, rather than taking her mind off her problems, it was unsettling her even more. What she needed was a nice love story, but the pile of new paperbacks had been moved from the room. The staff all seemed to have the idea that books belonged in the study, and she hadn't got around yet to asking them to leave her books in the bedroom.

She put the thriller down and just lay thinking for a while in the lamplight, but she still wasn't in any shape to fall asleep after the day's excitement, and finally she got up to go foraging for her books.

The house was in darkness, but probably if she put on a light a servant would appear from somewhere. She didn't want to disturb anyone; she knew her way. The courtyard was just lighted enough by the stars. She crossed the small courtyard and into the hallway that led to the larger one, and felt her way along the wall in semi-darkness.

She hadn't been nervous in the house before, but tonight she kept wondering if someone was keeping watch inside the house, too. The sense that eyes were watching her was disturbing, almost spooky, and for the first time she wondered if the place had ghosts.

Her nightshirt provided minimal cover. It was just a beige T-shirt she had torn the sleeves out of, covering her barely to mid-thigh. If there were men watching, Rosalind thought belatedly, she probably should have put on a robe. But the night air was pleasant on her bare skin, the tile floor was cool under her feet, soothing the lacerations she had got earlier. She went on.

She reached the third courtyard. It was in darkness, no light showing from the study, or the command centre, or whatever it was. She realized by the disappointment she felt that she had unconsciously been hoping to find Najib still there.

So he had decided to sleep somewhere else tonight. Her heart kicked a protest, and she shook her head. Paradise never did last, did it? The story of Adam and Eve, whatever else it was, was a metaphor for humanity's inability to inhabit perfection for long.

The door had an old-fashioned, wrought metal, latch-type handle, and Rosalind pushed it quietly down, trying not to make any noise. She didn't want some secret service type mistaking her for a house-breaker and giving her a karate chop to the neck or something.

It didn't give, and she tried again. Locked, she realized, and her heart thumped. Najib must be still in there, after all. She went to the window, but that was closed, too, though she was pretty sure no one ever closed the internal windows or locked the doors at night.

Rosalind heaved a sigh of irritation and turned away. She stepped straight into the embrace of the man standing behind her, and her heart jumped into another rhythm as his hands grasped her arms and held her away,

"What are you doing here?" Najib asked in a hoarse, strained voice, as if he was going through agony. "What do you want?"

Fourteen

His presence was enough to let her know that it was him she had come after. Whatever their arguments and misunderstandings of the day, she didn't want him sleeping in some other bed. Her body was softening with the grateful memory of delight. She needed him.

"I—I wanted a book."

"A book," he repeated tonelessly.

His upper body was bare—he was wearing only a pair of flowing white cotton trousers. She lifted her hands and pressed them against his chest. His skin was warm. She began to melt, like butter in the pan.

"Why haven't you come to bed?" she asked.

His breath kicked in his chest, and she smiled. Then his hands were tight on her arms, pushing her away.

"No, Rosalind," he said. "No, this will not work tonight. Tell me why you are trying to get into this room. Who do you want to call?"

His voice was a rasping whisper. He sounded like a dying man. He had watched and waited, knowing that tonight she would make some attempt. He had known, and still he had hoped it would be otherwise.

"Call?" she murmured, reaching for him. Why was he pushing her away, when she wanted to hold him and be held? She was lonely and hungry for him, she had had a terrible fright today, why wasn't he comforting her?

"Hold me," she said. "Najib, please hold me."

His arms were trembling with the effort not to wrap her against him. She reached for him again, and his grip weakened helplessly. Sensing it, she smiled and lifted her arms, sliding her hands up his chest and around his neck.

"Love me," she whispered, and was amazed to see an expression of agony cross his face.

"And what of tomorrow?" he whispered, through his teeth.

She didn't understand him, but she was past caring. "Never mind tomorrow," she pleaded. "Love me tonight."

He understood that he was lost. He bent and swung her up in his arms, and turned to trace the way back to the bedroom.

One last time. He would give her one last time to remember. A night of lovemaking she would remember and sigh for, all the rest of her life. And wish that she had been true.

The bedroom was as she had left it, one lamp glowing softly by the bed, the sheet flung aside. It seemed a closed, protected world all their own.

He set her on her feet and drew the T-shirt up over

her head in one continuous movement. Rosalind
gasped once to find herself so suddenly naked, and
then again, when she saw the passionate torment in
his face.

"Naj!" she cried softly.

"Yes," he said through his teeth, "yes, you will
cry my name tonight. I will remember the taste of you,
Rosalind, and how you called my name."

His hand caught in her hair, and drew her head
back, her face up for his kiss. She felt him tremble,
and the thought that he was struggling not to lose control ignited her. His mouth came down on hers with
wild hunger, his arm going around her back to press
her naked, sensitive breasts against his chest.

Heat burned all through her, her blood was molten
gold pouring down all the pathways of sensation. His
hand was around her waist, half lifting her off the
ground, her body bent backwards till she was dizzy,
his tongue driving hungrily inside the moist hollow of
her mouth.

He moved her just as he wished, tilting her head,
drawing her breasts against the roughness of his chest
hair, pressing her lower body against his hard, aroused
flesh, back and forth, melting her into readiness.

She reached for his powerfully aroused sex, but he
knocked her hand away. "No, my beauty," he said,
with a harshness she did not understand. "Tonight is
all for you."

Then she was being lowered through space as he
kissed her throat, her breasts, her stomach, and she felt
the cool tile floor under her feet, the bed under her
thighs and back.

His hands moved down her body and came to rest

on her thighs, and he dragged them apart and knelt on the floor between her knees. She sighed.

"Yes," he said, "yes, I know you like it, Rosalind. I give it to you to remember."

She felt the heat of his breath as he spoke, and had time for no more than a gasp of anticipation before the hot damp of his mouth pressed against her. He had learned what she liked in the days and nights past, and now he was ruthless with the knowledge he had gained. His tongue, his hands, his lips, were flames dancing over her, and she was helpless to do anything save accept the pleasure, flowing over her in drowning waves of liquid fire.

"Naj!" she cried, each time her body trembled in honeyed release. "Naj!"

And on and on, over and over, till she was weak.

At last he stood up, dragging the white cotton *shalwar* down his legs and off. Then she was being pulled up, her legs trembling, too weak. She would have protested that she could not stand, but he turned her to face away from him, and pushed her forward to bend down onto the high bed. And she was filled anew with sensation and anticipation.

Behind her, his knee pushed her knees wide apart, and now she was all open to him as his hands stroked her with rough, urgent, thrilling caress—thighs, hips, sex. His fingers gripped her hips, and the hungry pressure of him came tantalizingly between her thighs, once, twice. Then his hand cupped her sex to hold her for his thrust, and he entered that moist, hungry pathway of sensation with one long, strong stroke that took him to the hilt in her and sent almost unbearable sensation to every part of her. She cried out her shocked surprise from an open throat, and felt him swell to new hardness inside her.

He began to thrust into her, his hold on her hips drawing her back hard against him so that each thrust went to its depth, and this pleasure was so profound it was almost pain. She cried aloud with every thrust, and excitement mounted in her until mists shrouded her brain and she no longer knew where she was, or what she cried to him. Every stroke was too much, was not enough, was building to an explosion that she both feared and craved as he pushed his way in again and again past the million nerve ends of her being.

One hand released her hip, and then she felt his touch on that bud of nerves that was her centre, stroking, teasing, circling as the thrusts went on and on, sending sensation like fire roaring down her veins, across her skin, into her brain. She called, and begged, and cried to him, drunk with sensual delight and torment, until it suddenly exploded in her, and in him, spiralling out from somewhere deeper than herself to touch every greedy part of her. Then she sobbed his name again, and moaned, and the blackness enveloped her in waves.

He was already hard again, and lifting himself away, pushed her to lie on her back. He bent over her impatiently, pulling her legs apart, and she cried weakly at this new assault, "Oh, Naj, I don't think I can take any more."

"No more?" he growled. "No more? But you must have more, Rosalind, so that you will remember tonight always!"

Then he held her head in his two hands, bending over her. "Look at me, Rosalind!" he commanded, and obediently her eyes focussed and she smiled drunkenly up into dark, passionate, tormented eyes.

"Say my name."

The passion in his voice melted her all over again. Never in her life had she seen, or felt, such passionate hunger.

"Naj!" she said, and on the word he drove home in her, in one hard, powerful stroke. "Naj!" she cried again, and he heard how, in spite of being so sated, the need was building in her.

"No more?" he said, his hands tangling in her hair. He pounded into her unmercifully, and again pleasure built and exploded all around them.

Still it was not enough. His body surged into hunger again. He drew her up, lifted her high, and fitted himself to her again. She wrapped her legs around his waist, and her arms around his neck, and he carried her to the wall and leaned her back against it, his hands under her hips, his body locked with hers.

She reached out for the carafe of water on the table, and splashed some into her palm, wiping the cooling liquid over her hot face. Poured more, and wiped it over Naj's face, his chest.

He smiled. "More," he said. Obediently she splashed water on his chest, making him grunt, and over her own, over stomach and thighs, till the jug was empty. He bent his head to drink the water from her breast, and ripples of delicate sensation flowed to join the rivers already rushing through her.

He carried her along to the window, pulled open the lattice. A slight wind blew in, and they rested there, still conjoined, skin damp, letting it cool them as their bodies ground together. Outside the moon was high, casting ghostly white light over the world.

He cupped the mound of her breast in one hand, and kissed it in the moonlight, as somewhere, once, a worshipper had kissed the white marble breast of a goddess. Then he turned back to the bed, laid her down on it, moved up over her, and began again.

Everything was black. She had gone beyond the senses, beyond endurance, into a world where she was a tool for the expression of sexual pleasure, and she must submit to its will. Images of ancient statues occurred to her mind unbidden, the god and the goddess locked in sacred congress, and she understood them for the first time.

"Naj!" she whispered, for he, too, was an instrument of the Will.

He was above her, lifting and pounding into that seat of pleasure. Crying out with every thrust, so deep in her it seemed to reach her soul.

He knew that he was a fool. In his determination to drive her over the edge, he had only brought himself there. It was too deep in him now. She was a part of him forever, though he had intended it the other way. He would never forget her, or this night, as long as he lived.

He had to know. He could not go on in ignorance, loving her more and more deeply, hoping that she was worthy of his trust but not daring to trust. It would drive him mad, loving her like this, and yet so tormented by his fears.

"Rosalind," he said, his hand locking in her hair, his voice desperate, as he pushed helplessly in. "Rosalind, tell me the truth. You must tell me! Tell me! Tell me!"

She heard him through the cloud of delight that comes with complete submission to Will. Heard nothing but his voice in the raw, high cry of abandonment and pleasure, and it rasped along her nerves and added its weight to her joy.

He had lost control now. His body surged in her, and he knew this was the ultimate pleasure and there would be no holding back, there would be nothing left. He leaned down and pressed his lips to hers, and as it rocked through him, cried the anguish of unbearable pleasure against her mouth.

She cried his name then, exactly as he had intended. But he also cried hers.

"Approach," the sultan commanded.

The portrait drew her. She came nearer, while the old sultan's eyes followed her. He lifted his hand, and she bent and kissed the ring.

Her mouth burned from the contact. She drew back, staring at the pink stone. She stared closer, closer.

"Oh!" Rosalind exclaimed aloud.

Rosalind awoke aching in every muscle, but with her cells so stuffed with honey it didn't matter. Feeling his hand stroke her spine, she purred in gratitude and rolled over. Najib was lying on his side, his elbow propping up his head, watching her. The sheet was draped over his hips, leaving his powerful chest and arms naked for her delectation.

There was a frown behind his dark gaze.

"Good morning," she murmured. His hand cupped her breast, trailed up to her lower lip, where his thumb first brushed her, and then his mouth.

"Tell me, Rosalind," he begged, and it was as if the words were torn from him against his will.

She closed her eyes against the wave of feeling, and

knew that she was safe. She wanted to say it—they were words it seemed she had been wanting to say to him for a whole lifetime. *I love you.*

She heaved a sigh, and a smile played across her lips. "What do you want to hear?"

"The truth!" he said violently. "I cannot bear to live with lies another day!"

Rosalind gasped. "What?"

Bitterness rose up in his throat as he looked at her. Only now, loving Rosalind, did he understand how pale had been his feeling for Maysa. At the time he had believed the confusion of guilt and desire must be love, but now he understood that the pain he had felt when he walked in to find her in bed with another man had been the pain of bruised pride.

Rosalind's betrayal of him would cut him in two. Losing her, he would lose half himself.

And how much more power she had to betray him than Maysa had had. Maysa, with her simple greed, heartlessly turning everything in life to her own advantage, was a baby compared to the games Rosalind must be playing with them all.

He had learned it all too late. He was lost now. He should never have agreed to this charade. His own weakness had been clear from the outset. What misplaced vanity had allowed him to believe he could live in such close confines with this woman and remain aloof?

Jamshid had already proved her powers. Grasping at the straw of her pregnancy to bind Rosalind to him, against every family duty…leaving her his fortune, the jewel that was his only because he was his grandfather's heir…these were the acts of a man besotted. Naj himself should have seen this as a warning.

Now she was playing for some deeper prize, but although he could guess, he could not be certain what she really wanted. Perhaps she was only afraid.

Some part of him wanted to believe that he could turn her from her course. That his clear sexual hold over her would also give him some hold over her emotions, even if it could never equal the power of her hold over him.

He leaned to kiss her as she gazed at him aghast, but she turned her face away.

"Tell me!"

"You said that last night. *Tell me the truth,* you said. I remember."

She sat up, her brain buzzing, pulling the sheet to her breasts. "You were trying to get me into a sexual frenzy in the hopes that I would confess in the heat of the moment? Is that what you were trying to do?" She closed her eyes as thoughts took shape. "You were just trying to—this has all been an attempt to manipulate me, hasn't it? All of it. You've been using sex— pretending to be attached to Sam…acting just like a spy! Are you a spy?"

He gazed at her.

"Your men, you said," she recalled, her heart clenching with painful spasms. "My God, a spy! And as Cup Companion—I suppose you actually run the secret service or something!"

"So you know that much," he observed levelly. "How do you know?"

"You think I got the news from Ghasib?" Rosalind shrank away from him.

"Tell me the truth," he begged.

"You know what? You're such a cheat yourself you wouldn't know the truth if it lay down in front of you and offered its belly. I have told you—and this is the last time I am ever going to say it, so listen carefully—I have told you nothing but the truth from start to finish. I have never lied to you. And if you had any humanity in you at all, you would know it.''

''What you have told me defies science.''

''Maybe it does. Sometimes, when you accept what seems to defy science, you come upon truth, don't you? You of all people should know that!''

''Should I?''

''A plane defies science unless you understand the science that puts it up in the air,'' she said. ''A *bumblebee* defies science every time it flies, and I guess it will go on doing so even if no one ever discovers the science that proves that a bumblebee is capable of flying. Mohammad defied science, too, didn't he, when he split the moon in two for all those people who couldn't believe?''

''Are you saying Sam's birth was a miracle?''

''No, no miracle. I'm merely pointing out that when it suits you, you accept things that defy science. Either because of personal observation, or because of faith. Your personal observation of me could have told you I was telling the truth, and if you had even a little faith in me as a person, that would have told you, too.''

She was not making the best logic, but still his raised eyebrow angered her.

''But you don't have any faith in me. You made love to me and all this time you've believed…that you were making love to Ghasib's spy in the al Jawadi camp? Do you know what kind of person that makes you?'' she said, with a disdain that seared him.

''You've made one big mistake, Najib, and I'm sure that kind of blind spot is bad news for a spy.''

He laughed, but without mirth. "Yes," he agreed. "I made one big mistake, and this kind of blind spot is very bad news for a spy."

"You started from the assumption that I was lying. In order to make that fit, you've had to jump to ridiculous, far-fetched, spy novel conclusions...and you had to act like a villain with me. None of that was necessary. All you had to do was trust me. I have never seen your damned al Jawadi Rose. I have not given birth to the next heir. All you had to do was be willing to believe that I was telling you the truth."

"And what then?"

"Then you wouldn't have had to go to all the trouble of making love to me from a cold heart," Rosalind said bitterly, slipping off the end of the bed as tears burned her throat. "You didn't have to pretend passion for me to get the truth, Najib. That was all just your spy's fantasy. You already had the truth, right from day one."

Words leapt to his lips, but he held them back. He wanted to say that his heart had never been cold, but he was too close to telling her everything. His judgement was unsound. He could not afford to make any mistakes or let his heart rule.

She stood for a moment looking down at him. "Well, you won't do it anymore," she promised, turned and went into the bathroom, and closed and locked the door.

But there was one thing she hadn't told the truth about, even if she hadn't realized it till now. She had seen the al Jawadi Rose. Jamshid *had* given it to her.

The dream had made her see what was right in front of her nose.

Fifteen

"**O**h, that's wonderful, Kamila!" Princess Zara exclaimed, as the ruby-and-diamond star was pinned into Rosalind's hair. "That's the perfect touch!"

The Princess of East Barakat was stretched out on a divan, her elbow on a huge silk pillow, her young baby asleep in his bassinet beside her, watching avidly as her favourite designer tweaked the folds of Rosalind's wedding outfit.

They had flown to Prince Rafi's palace the same afternoon. On their arrival Rosalind had learned that the wedding would take place in two days. At Zara's hands she had been pitchforked into the preparations so quickly she had no leisure for deciding whether to call a halt or not.

But even if she had had the leisure, she wouldn't have had the courage once she saw how much planning had taken place. The palace was already filled with wedding guests. Every second person she was introduced to was a prince or princess. Rosalind knew she couldn't do it.

Anyway, what reason did she have? What had changed since she had told them she would do it? Najib had never pretended to believe her, or implied that he would come to love her. She had learned nothing new. It was only that her hopes had died.

"And flowers to match," murmured the designer.

"Kamila is having a Paris show this autumn," Zara told Rosalind. "This blend she does of Eastern and Western styles is just so unique. We're convinced it's going to be a terrific success, and your wedding being covered by *Hello!* will be the perfect launch, won't it, Kamila?"

"*Insha'Allah,*" Kamila agreed with a grin.

Rosalind was watching her own reflection in the mirror. The outfit was a creamy white that suited her tanned skin and sun-bleached hair beautifully, but the colour was the only thing about it that spoke of the traditional Western wedding dress.

It was composed of a full-length coat with small upstanding collar, worn over the traditional Eastern tunic dress and trousers, all in the same milky silk. Running down each side of the front opening and around the collar were panels of fabulously delicate embroidery in red, green and gold reminiscent of the decoration of an illuminated Quran. The embroidery was repeated in a broad band around the ankles of the trousers. Medium-heel mules in the softest white leather for her feet, and around her shoulders and head a finely woven white scarf.

In her hair, the "something borrowed" from Zara. The two women were meeting for the first time, although Zara had been overseeing the design of Rosalind's wedding dress for days. She was very anxious that Rosalind should like the result.

"I love it!" Rosalind said. The effect was striking and unusual, and Rosalind could imagine that Kamila was going to be a raging success in Europe, and said so.

"They call Kamila's stuff 'intensely wearable' in the fashion pages back home, don't they, Kamila?" Zara said. "We haven't worked out yet whether that's a dart or a laurel."

Rosalind laughed and, the outfit approved and the fitting done, the designer helped her take it off. When it was all in its bags again, along with several outfits for "the honeymoon," the two women were left alone, lounging in the pretty sitting room that was part of Zara's private apartments. It had a balcony overlooking a garden that, because of the climate in the mountains, was more like an English garden than Rosalind would ever have imagined possible so far from home.

"Are you nervous?" asked Zara, reaching into the bassinet beside her and lifting out her baby, who had awakened and was beginning to make himself heard.

"Yes," Rosalind said bluntly.

"I'm sure you're doing the right thing, Rosalind," Zara said. "You don't need to worry about Naj not keeping his word. You can trust him completely." Zara was warming to her theme. "I work with Najib, so I happen to know."

"You work with him?"

"Najib supervises the National Museum and a couple of smaller ones. He does a lot of work in the West, trying to convince governments who accepted pillaged works in the eighteenth and nineteenth—and twentieth!—centuries to give or sell the stuff back to us. He and Gazi work together quite often—Gazi handles all our publicity—so I see a lot of Naj. I'm organizing the new Alexander the Great wing that's going to house all the stuff from the dig at Iskandiyar.''

Rosalind gazed at her. "I do know he's a spy, Zara. Do you mean the museum work is his cover?"

"Unh-unh." Zara shook her head. "He's not a career spy, I know that much. The Cup Companions all do whatever is necessary at times, and at the moment the game's afoot, as old Sherlock used to say. There are certain affairs of state Rafi's not telling me at the moment—but I think it's tied up with Ghasib. Everybody's pulling out all the stops, and Najib's war experience probably makes him invaluable."

"Oh," Rosalind remarked quietly.

"You know Najib was in the Kaljuk War?"

"Yes, he mentioned it."

"When he heard that Prince Omar was forming the Company of Cup Companions, he told Rafi he wanted to go with him. His father was a Parvani, you know, and he's related to the Durranis on that side."

The baby interrupted with an imperative request for a meal. Zara cooed and kissed as she opened her shirt and fitted him to her breast, then looked up at Rosalind with a contented smile.

"Did you breastfeed Sam?" she asked.

Rosalind swallowed. "No, I...I'd have liked to, but I couldn't."

"Aw, that's too bad," Zara commiserated. "Maybe with your next."

"I hope so."

The baby was suddenly asleep. Rosalind watched with a smile as Zara moved to disengage him from

her breast, and only sparked a return to ferocious suck-
ing.

"It's going to be a major exclusive—the first inte-
rior photos of Prince Rafi's palace, *and* a Cup Companion's romantic remarriage to his lost wife," Zara
said. "The magazine's paying a huge amount for the
privilege, to the Parvan War Relief fund, because, as
Gazi says, if they didn't have to pay for the privilege
they wouldn't value it. He wants the best possible
spread."

No, she couldn't possibly call a halt.

"I have something to tell you," Rosie said.

"And I have something to tell you," Naj said. He
took her hand and turned to lead her along the path.
Overhead the stars were bright, and the moon glowed
on the peak of Mount Shir far away. They climbed a
little, and then sat on a crag, looking down over the
palace. It sparkled with lights.

"Shall I speak first, Rosalind? I want to say I am
sorry. You were very right, I made a mistake when I
took it for granted that you must be telling some lie.
And as soon as I looked at what you had told me,
believing and accepting that you told me nothing but
the truth, I saw the truth. The only thing that answers
every question."

"Did you?" she whispered.

"I understand, too, why you could not tell me the
story yourself. I am a fool, Rosalind. It is so obvious.
Lamis is the answer, is she not?

"Samir is my own sister's child."

Rosalind and Lamis had always been friendly, and
they were drawn closer together by the death of Jam-

shid. Rosie had been aware that Lamis was worried by something, though Lamis never spoke of it. But when the letter arrived from Jamshid's grandfather, Lamis no longer needed to bear her load alone. "Now you will understand, Rosalind. Now you know what I am facing," she had said, by way of preface.

She told Rosalind the horrible story she had been keeping to herself for months: the man she had loved, who said he understood and respected her religious principles, had raped her. She was pregnant. And she had denied the pregnancy until it was a reality that could be denied no longer.

Shame and fear together tortured her. Her grandfather...she did not know how far his anger would take him. And she was starting to show. She was resigned to giving her baby up for adoption, but urgently now, she had to find a way to keep any whisper of her pregnancy from her family. But London was a hub, and had so many eyes.

Rosalind, product of a modern Western upbringing, with no real understanding of Lamis's background, would, a few days before, have indignantly urged her to tell her family the bitter truth, because how could anyone possibly blame her? But not since the letter. Now Rosalind understood that at all costs Lamis must protect herself from her grandfather's ugly rage.

Both of them were crazy with their griefs, and no doubt that was why they never looked at possible consequences when the wild plan occurred to the two friends. It appeared so breathtakingly simple and brilliant a solution that they simply never questioned it: Lamis would have her child under Rosalind's name.

Rosalind would take a few months' leave of absence from her job at the Parvan Embassy, which would surprise no one. Lamis meanwhile was researching her thesis and could take time away without causing comment. They would go to a city in the north, where no one knew them and the Middle Eastern population was high.

Lamis would go to the doctor under Rosalind's name, register the birth under Rosalind's name, and give the child up for adoption. Simple.

And it worked. The two girls kept very much to themselves in their apartment in the teeming heart of Birmingham. Although she hadn't previously worn chador in her life, Lamis never went into the street without her face veiled, and when she visited the overworked National Health doctor in their neighbourhood under Rosalind's name and told him that she was a widow, he had tacitly understood that she was lying to save herself from shame, but with no idea what the lie really was.

Rosalind was Lamis's birth assistant. She gave birth at home with a midwife, a choice common enough to be unremarkable. The birth was straightforward and uncomplicated.

And all according to plan. Until the two friends looked at their beautiful baby and could not give him up....

"She made me promise not to keep in touch," Rosie told Najib now. "It killed her to leave him, though she knew she had no choice."

When the time came for Lamis to go home, she had wept over her baby with terrifying ferocity. And then she had asked Rosie one last favour. "Don't call me, Rosie, don't write, don't stay in touch," she had begged, emotion choking her, as she packed her bags. "I have to put him out of my mind. I'll go crazy if I think of him. I'll have to lie and pretend to everyone I know, and I can't live two lives. It would kill me.''

Rosie had forgotten, too. In her heart, Sam had become her own son.

''I have something to tell you,'' Rosie said a few minutes later, as the moon rose higher over the mountains. ''I was wrong. I'm pretty sure Jamshid did give me the al Jawadi Rose.''

''*What?*'' Naj exclaimed.

''Jamshid told me it was rose crystal. It's in a little carved wooden stand that looks as if it was made in India. He said it was an old family heirloom with sentimental value. He made me promise that if he died in the war I'd always keep it and give it to his son as a memento of him when he was older.''

He was staring at her, speechless.

''Where—where is it now?'' he croaked.

''It's sitting on my coffee table, Naj. Right beside that little rose of Lamis's that you were looking at that day. You almost had your hand on it.''

''Sam,'' said Rosalind, ''this is your Aunt Lamis.''

She had been deeply nervous when she learned of Lamis's arrival at the palace for the wedding, but the moment she saw her friend again it was all right. Lamis hugged her tightly, smiling and crying together, and saying, ''Oh, Rosie!'' over and over.

She had asked to meet her son, and they had gone to Zara's private apartments for the meeting.

''Hello,'' Sam said shyly, hiding behind Rosalind.

''Oh, he looks just like Grandfather!'' Lamis exclaimed. ''Hello, Samir.''

She held out her arms. Sam looked at Rosalind, and

she smiled, so he stepped towards Lamis. She put her arms lightly around him and gazed down at him. "Oh, what a darling you are!" She kissed his cheek with a restraint that was painful to watch.

She looked at her friend. "Thank you, Rosie. What can words express? Has it been all right? I can see by looking that he's happy." She bent and kissed Sam again, lightly, not frightening him with too much feeling, and let him go.

He stood for a moment frowning in thought, gazing at her. "Why are you my aunt?"

"Because I'm your new daddy's sister," Lamis said, wiping a tear from her eye. She sniffed. "And I love you. I love you very much, and I always will."

On the eve of their wedding, Rosalind and Najib walked alone.

"What proved it to you?" Rosalind asked.

"You did, with what you said."

She smiled, her eyes hot with unshed tears. "Really?"

"When I trusted that you had told me the truth about everything, the solution was obvious. Like one of those visual puzzles that suddenly becomes some other image. But even if I hadn't seen the truth about Lamis, I saw the truth about you. The truth that you were an honourable woman. Even if I had seen no further than that, it was suddenly clear to me."

She was choking with hope, and too moved to speak, and they walked amongst the flowers and fountains, the beautiful scalloped arches, the marble pillars, the trees, as the sun set behind the mountains, casting cool, delicious shadow.

Najib was magnificent in the costume of the mountain men who were his forebears—loose trousers and a long tunic top, with a richly embroidered waistcoat on top. He reminded her of the photographs she had seen of the Parvan fighters.

"You've talked to Lamis?" she asked.

"We had a long talk this afternoon. It was a relief to her to be able to tell me. It was a relief she could have had at the time, but she was too afraid of my grandfather to see it."

"Would you have helped her?"

He glanced down with bemused eyes. "What else, Rosie? Do you imagine that, like my grandfather, I would have blamed her for the man's vicious crime?"

"Sometimes what you said to me wasn't very far off what your grandfather said," she reminded him softly.

He acknowledged it with a rueful grimace. "I am sorry, Rosie, my beautiful Rose. One day I will tell you about the woman I judged you by, instead of judging you for yourself. Instead of seeing you as you were, I looked at you through my experience of Maysa. And even when I wanted most to trust you, my loyalty to others meant I had to assume the worst, to take the gravest precautions. I had to distrust myself."

"Lamis told me she thinks the family is gearing up for some kind of attempt to regain the throne, and that's why it's all so critical."

"She is right. But this is a secret that must be mentioned to no one, Rosalind."

"The two men I met at Sir John's—are they the sons of Prince Wafiq?"

"Ashraf was my grandfather's choice to sit on the restored throne. He is the family's choice, too. He is the eldest son of my Uncle Wafiq. We fought together on many campaigns and conceived our plans then.''

''And is that why you were so horrified to discover Sam's existence?''

''There were many reasons why the belated discovery of a son of Kamil was an unwelcome surprise. The first being that, as our plans progressed, his existence was bound to be discovered by Ghasib's agents. We had to move instantly to protect him, and that had its own risks. There was also the problem of the al Jawadi Rose. My grandfather made Ashraf his heir, but the ring was then missing. Ghasib might easily have set your son up against Ashraf in an attempt to divide the people. In such a situation, the Rose would be of huge importance.

''But our campaign is already well under way. It would have caused very grave results if we had tried to stop it now. Things are going to be gradually revealed over the next few weeks. There is no effective way to stop the revelations from occurring. To try would only be to put lives in danger.''

''Are you saying Ghasib's days are numbered in weeks?'' she asked breathlessly.

''We hope so. But you must wipe this information from your mind, Rosalind. Do not even think of it in the privacy of your own mind. The news must not escape.''

She frowned at a thought. ''When Lamis and I registered Sam's birth…she must have known that it was possible that one day people would find out and believe he was Prince Kamil's son.''

''She knew, but thought it remote. But she felt— and she is right, Rosalind!—that there was no reason her son should not inherit his great-grandfather's throne. It is a stupid prejudice we have about the male line. She said to me, *Nobody wants to remember that Mohammad had no sons! All the line of descent from the Prophet originally came through his daughter. Why is descent through the mother now meaningless? At least we know for certain who a child's mother is!*"

"Oh, she *has* changed!" Rosalind said on a breathless laugh. "She would never have said that five years ago!"

"And she is right. Even if, in this particular case, her argument is somewhat disproved by our own experience."

They laughed a little at that.

"You see, we were going to give Sam up for adoption," Rosalind said. "And she wanted him to have a lead to his rightful family if, when he grew up, he ever searched his background. If he found me, I promised I'd tell him the truth. But what if he didn't find me? What if I died before he found me? That was why we registered the birth as we did."

He stopped and turned to face her. "You did a brave thing, Rosalind, taking a child to raise on your own. This is not a thing many women would do."

"You don't know how heartbroken I was," she said. "Sam was such a comfort. I've never regretted what I did.

"And Lamis certainly made sure I had a financially easy time of it," she continued, before he could speak. "She bought the apartment—did she tell you that was why she pretended to have gambling losses?—and she bought bonds to pay his school fees. We both wanted me to be able to be a stay-at-home mother."

He shook his head. "But the burden of being both

father and mother to a child, Rosalind, nothing lifted this from you.''

His eyes were searching, and her heart began to beat in slow, heavy thuds. ''No,'' she whispered.

''Rosalind, we are to be married in the morning. When we agreed to this, it was not meant to be real. But I love you the way a man hopes to love the woman he makes his wife.''

She sighed a sigh of completion and homecoming. ''Do you, Najib?''

''I loved you from the moment I saw you—no, before that! When I looked at your photograph, I knew then that you were the woman for me. I was jealous— do you believe it? I looked at your picture and I was jealous of my cousin because five years ago you had smiled at him like that.''

She could say nothing, only listen.

''Tomorrow when I take my vows I will mean it. I want to marry you, and be a father to your son. I want it to be real for you, too, Rosalind. I want to hear you say you can love me!''

Her heart stopped beating so that she could listen in perfect stillness.

''Will you marry me, my Rose?'' said Najib.

They were married in the morning, when the mountain air was crisp and delicious, in the palace's Rose Garden. It had been planted over fifty years ago, as the magazine afterwards explained to its readers, by Prince Rafi's late stepmother, Queen Azizah.

Now it boasted every variety of rose, the sweet-scented and the merely beautiful, climbers, shrubs, trees. There were banks and walls and arched trellises of roses—purple, red, pink, white and yellow.

To add to the magic, Rosalind's lovely, trailing bouquet was composed of red and white roses from the garden, picked only last night. It matched the beautiful diamond-and-ruby "something borrowed" pin in her hair, a loan from Princess Zara, who afterwards made the bride a gift of the fabulous star.

The bride was accompanied to the altar by the wedding couple's own son, Samir. The boy dressed in the Eastern pyjama outfit called *shalwar kamees,* in richly coloured silk brocade that matched the bride's embroidery.

Sheikh Najib, the Cup Companion to Prince Rafi well-known in the West for his attempts to repatriate the famous so-called Cup of Cyrus, now in the Louvre, and several statues and a plate residing in the British Museum, was magnificently regal in gold and ruby.

The guest list was small but significant, with Prince Rafi and Princess Zara heading up a glittering elite that included Prince Omar and Princess Jana from Central Barakat, Prince Karim and Princess Caroline from West Barakat, Crown Prince Kavian and Princess Alinor from Parvan, and Sheikh Arash al Khosravi and his new wife, Sheikha Lana, the daughter of American computer mogul Jonathan Holding, as well as the groom's sister, now revealed as the granddaughter of Sultan Hafzuddin, Sheikha Lamis al Makhtoum, and her husband....

A delicious rumour ran through the crowd that the heirs of the old Sultan of Bagestan were also in the congregation to see their cousin married, but if so, no one was sure who they might be. Although Najib al Makhtoum had gallantly revealed himself in order to re-marry, under his own name, the woman he had first married five years ago, it was safe only because he was not considered to be in the direct line to the throne. The actual heirs of Hafzuddin al Jawadi could not risk being unveiled, the magazine explained. Many in the ancient, noble family had paid for their ancestry with their lives since the bloody 1969 coup that had put the man the tabloids were calling Ghastly Ghasib in power in Bagestan....

Rosalind scarcely noticed the photographers, so nervous was she as she walked down the flower-strewn carpet of grass towards the white canopy where Najib awaited her. He was breathtakingly handsome in the gold and red robes, the rich, jewelled turban. He looked like something out of a picture book.

But best of all was the expression in his eyes. Najib was looking at her with such a mixture of love, pride, hunger and happiness in his face that her heart soared.

Accompanied by her son, Rosalind moved to stand beside her proud sheikh, knowing that they had come home at last.

Epilogue

The door was opened, when he rang, by a white-haired woman.

"You are Helen Mitchell?"

"I am."

"Good afternoon. My name is Haroun al Muntazir. I believe my cousin Rosalind telephoned you earlier."

The woman stared at him, her mouth open. "Oh, my goodness!" she exclaimed. "Oh, yes, she did, but—"

His eyebrows went up. "Did she not ask you to let me pick up a certain ornament?"

"Yes, she—I mean, she said, 'He'll take the rose crystal ornament,' but—who was that who came earlier, then?"

He stiffened. "Came earlier?"

"Yes, I thought it was…oh dear! He said, I am here to take the rose.…"

Haroun went still. "And you—" He swallowed. "You gave it to him?"

"Well, he came in—well, yes. I mean, I thought it was the right thing to do. He seemed to know exactly what he wanted. I thought he was the man Rosalind had sent. Was it terribly important? I'm awfully sorry, but it was almost an hour ago. I don't know if you could catch him."

"Oh, I will catch him, Mrs. Mitchell, be sure of that." Haroun bent his head in a bow. "It will perhaps take time, but I will catch him."

*   *   *   *   *

Silhouette® *Desire* is proud to present

SONS OF THE DESERT

THE SULTANS

Powerful sheikhs born to rule and destined to find love as eternal as the sands.

In three breathtakingly sensual new romances, Alexandra Sellers continues her bestselling series, Sons of the Desert. Love and adventure are the destiny of the three grandsons of the late Sultan of Bagestan, who must fight to overthrow a ruthless dictator and restore the sultanate.

Look for these exciting stories:

The Sultan's Heir
(Desire #1379—July 2001)

Undercover Sultan
(Desire #1385—August 2001)

Sleeping with the Sultan
(Desire #1391—September 2001)

Available at your favorite retail outlet.

Where love comes alive™

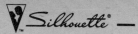

Feel like a star with Silhouette.

We will fly you and a guest to New York City for an
exciting weekend stay at a glamorous 5-star hotel.
Experience a refreshing day at one of New York's
trendiest spas and have your photo taken by a
professional. Plus, receive $1,000 U.S. spending money!

Flowers...long walks...dinner for two... how does Silhouette Books make romance come alive for you?

Send us a script, with 500 words or less, along with visuals (only drawings,
magazine cutouts or photographs or combination thereof). Show us how
Silhouette Makes Your Love Come Alive. Be creative and have fun. No
purchase necessary. All entries must be clearly marked with your name,
address and telephone number. All entries will become property of
Silhouette and are not returnable. **Contest closes September 28, 2001.**

Please send your entry to: **Silhouette Makes You a Star!**

In U.S.A.
P.O. Box 9069
Buffalo, NY, 14269-9069

In Canada
P.O. Box 637
Fort Erie, ON, L2A 5X3

Look for contest details on the next page, by visiting www.eHarlequin.com or
request a copy by sending a self-addressed envelope to the applicable address
above. Contest open to Canadian and U.S. residents who are 18 or over.
Void where prohibited.

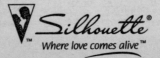

Our lucky winner's photo will appear in a Silhouette ad. Join the fun!

SRMYAS1

HARLEQUIN "SILHOUETTE MAKES YOU A STAR!" CONTEST 1308
OFFICIAL RULES
NO PURCHASE NECESSARY TO ENTER

1. To enter, follow directions published in the offer to which you are responding. Contest begins June 1, 2001, and ends on September 28, 2001. Entries must be postmarked by September 28, 2001, and received by October 5, 2001. Enter by hand-printing (or typing) on an 8 ½" x 11" piece of paper your name, address (including zip code), contest number/name and attaching a script containing 500 words or less, along with drawings, photographs or magazine cutouts, or combinations thereof (i.e., collage) on no larger than 9" x 12" piece of paper, describing how the Silhouette books make romance come alive for you. Mail via first-class mail to: Harlequin "Silhouette Makes You a Star!" Contest 1308, (in the U.S.) P.O. Box 9069, Buffalo, NY 14269-9069, (in Canada) P.O. Box 637, Fort Erie, Ontario, Canada L2A 5X3. Limit one entry per person, household or organization.

2. Contests will be judged by a panel of members of the Harlequin editorial, marketing and public relations staff. Fifty percent of criteria will be judged against script and fifty percent will be judged against drawing, photographs and/or magazine cutouts. Judging criteria will be based on the following:

   - Sincerity—25%
   - Originality and Creativity—50%
   - Emotionally Compelling—25%

   In the event of a tie, duplicate prizes will be awarded. Decisions of the judges are final.

3. All entries become the property of Torstar Corp. and may be used for future promotional purposes. Entries will not be returned. No responsibility is assumed for lost, late, illegible, incomplete, inaccurate, nondelivered or misdirected mail.

4. Contest open only to residents of the U.S. (except Puerto Rico) and Canada who are 18 years of age or older, and is void wherever prohibited by law; all applicable laws and regulations apply. Any litigation within the Province of Quebec respecting the conduct or organization of a publicity contest may be submitted to the Régie des alcools, des courses et des jeux for a ruling. Any litigation respecting the awarding of a prize may be submitted to the Régie des alcools, des courses et des jeux only for the purpose of helping the parties reach a settlement. Employees and immediate family members of Torstar Corp. and D. L. Blair, Inc., their affiliates, subsidiaries and all other agencies, entities and persons connected with the use, marketing or conduct of this contest are not eligible to enter. Taxes on prizes are the sole responsibility of the winner. Acceptance of any prize offered constitutes permission to use winner's name, photograph or other likeness for the purposes of advertising, trade and promotion on behalf of Torstar Corp., its affiliates and subsidiaries without further compensation to the winner, unless prohibited by law.

5. Winner will be determined no later than November 30, 2001, and will be notified by mail. Winner will be required to sign and return an Affidavit of Eligibility/Release of Liability/Publicity Release form within 15 days after winner notification. Noncompliance within that time period may result in disqualification and an alternative winner may be selected. All travelers must execute a Release of Liability prior to ticketing and must possess required travel documents (e.g., passport, photo ID) where applicable. Trip must be booked by December 31, 2001, and completed within one year of notification. No substitution of prize permitted by winner. Torstar Corp. and D. L. Blair, Inc., their parents, affiliates and subsidiaries are not responsible for errors in printing of contest, entries and/or game pieces. In the event of printing or other errors that may result in unintended prize values or duplication of prizes, all affected game pieces or entries shall be null and void. **Purchase or acceptance of a product offer does not improve your chances of winning.**

6. Prizes: (1) Grand Prize—A 2-night/3-day trip for two (2) to New York City, including round-trip coach air transportation nearest winner's home and hotel accommodations (double occupancy) at The Plaza Hotel, a glamorous afternoon makeover at a trendy New York spa, $1,000 in U.S. spending money and an opportunity to have a professional photo taken and appear in a Silhouette advertisement (approximate retail value: $7,000). (10) Ten Runner-Up Prizes of gift packages (retail value $50 ea.). Prizes consist of only those items listed as part of the prize. Limit one prize per person. Prize is valued in U.S. currency.

7. For the name of the winner (available after December 31, 2001) send a self-addressed, stamped envelope to: Harlequin "Silhouette Makes You a Star!" Contest 1197 Winners, P.O. Box 4200 Blair, NE 68009-4200 or you may access the www.eHarlequin.com Web site through February 28, 2002.

Contest sponsored by Torstar Corp., P.O Box 9042, Buffalo, NY 14269-9042.

SRMYAS2

COMING NEXT MONTH

#1381 HARD TO FORGET—Annette Broadrick

Man of the Month

Although Joe Sanchez hadn't seen Elena Moldonado in over ten years, he'd never forgotten his high school sweetheart. Now that Elena was back in town, Joe wanted her back in *his* arms. The stormy passion between them proved as wild as ever, but Joe would have to regain Elena's trust before he'd have a chance at the love of a lifetime.

#1382 A LOVING MAN—Cait London

Rose Granger didn't want to have a thing to do with worldly and sophisticated Stefan Donatien! She preferred her life just as it was, without the risk of heartbreak. Besides, what could the handsome Stefan possibly see in a simple small-town woman? But Stefan's tender seductions were irresistible, and Rose found herself wishing he would stay…forever.

#1383 HAVING HIS CHILD—Amy J. Fetzer

Wife, Inc./The Baby Bank

With no husband in sight and her biological clock ticking, Angela Justice figured the local sperm bank was the only way to make her dreams of having a baby come true. That was before Angela's best friend, Dr. Lucas Ryder, discovered her plans and decided to grant her wish—the old-fashioned way!

#1384 BABY OF FORTUNE—Shirley Rogers

Fortunes of Texas: The Lost Heirs

Upon discovering that he was an heir to the famed Fortune clan, Justin Bond resolved to give his marriage a second chance. His estranged wife, Heather, was more than willing to welcome Justin back into her life. But would Justin welcome Heather back into his heart when he learned the secret his wife had kept from him?

#1385 UNDERCOVER SULTAN—Alexandra Sellers

Sons of the Desert: The Sultans

When corporate spy Mariel de Vouvray was forced into an uneasy partnership with Sheikh Haroun al Jawadi, her powerful attraction to him didn't make things any easier! With every new adventure, Mariel fell further under the spell of her seductive sheikh, and soon she longed to make their partnership into something far more permanent.

#1386 BEAUTY IN HIS BEDROOM—Ashley Summers

Clint Whitfield came home after two years overseas and found feisty Regina Flynn living in his mansion. His first instinct was to throw the lovely strawberry blond intruder off his property—and out of his life. His second instinct was to let her stay—and to persuade the delectable Gina *into* his bedroom!

SDCNM0701